The Rainbow Frog & The Mad Scientist

The Adventures of Caroline and Euni:
Book One

Written By:

Joshua S Joseph

Illustrated By:

Chia Americo

The Rainbow Frog & The Mad Scientist

Author: Joshua S Joseph
Illustrations: Chia Americo
See final page in the book for additional and contact information
Color Illustrations: JSJoseph.com/CarolineEuni1/Illustrations

Second Edition, 2020, United States of America

Book One in the book series: The Adventures of Caroline and Euni

ISBN: 9781656638434

For my girls.

*See last page for information about
the author and the illustrator*

Part 1: The Rainbow Frog

Chapter 1

Once upon a time, in a time not too different from mine and yours - and, come to think of it, in a place not too different from mine and yours - there lived a young, bright, feisty girl, whose name happened to be Caroline.

Yes, Caro*line*, rhymes with *mine*, even if her sister (whose name happened to be Cora) called her Caro*lyn*, rhymes with *grin.* This, in turn, led to their pet unicorn, Euni, also calling her Carolyn, since she learned the sisters' names by listening to the two of them. But now we're well ahead of ourselves, aren't we? We should, I think, start at the beginning - after all, what other place is there to start?

This clever and adventurous Caroline, nine years old at the beginning of our story, loved the outdoors. Spent every moment she could, in fact, playing in the forest behind her home. She loved exploring, inventing silly imaginary games, and getting dirty. Caroline even loved getting lost and having to find her way home.

She always, of course, found her way home.

But more than anything else in the whole world (well, other than her family), Caroline loved animals. She loved any and all animals, loved to find them and look at them and feel them and play with them - so she was often sad about her father's rule against having any animals in their house.

And if you asked Caroline what animals were her favorites, she would answer that her favorites were the weird looking animals (the stranger the better), and unicorns. She didn't believe, then, that unicorns actually existed, but they were still her favorites, along with animals with crazy eyes and too many legs and weird antennae.

One day, Caroline was playing by the creek in the forest behind her home, stomping her pink rain boots in the mud beside the water. She sang a quiet song to herself as she played, a song about dragonflies and ladybugs, and was playing an imaginary game where she was discovering a new world in that creek, a world full of strange creatures that needed her help. She didn't believe, then, that new worlds actually existed, but it was still fun to imagine.

After closely inspecting a giant spider web (pretending she saved the spider's home from an evil witch), and then saying hi to a few birds in the trees above (pretending they were giant people-eating birds that she had to make friends with), Caroline noticed a strange looking frog in the mud by the creek. While there were always a lot of frogs around the creek, most were plain and boring and just a dirty green color. But this small frog, barely visible in the light brown mud, had a shimmering rainbow on its back that caught Caroline's attention.

"Well isn't that strange," Caroline said to herself, smiling, as she approached the frog. The frog didn't hop away, like Caroline worried it might, but instead just looked right up at her with large, intelligent eyes as she inspected its back.

"You have the most beautiful color pattern!" Caroline said to the frog. "I've never seen such a rainbow on a frog! Or any animal, really!"

To this the frog croaked, cheerfully, while still staring into Caroline's eyes. Caroline giggled at the frog's noise.

Soon mesmerized by the sparkling rainbow on the frog, Caroline decided to try and pick it up. Reaching down, Caroline was again surprised that the rainbow frog didn't try to hop away, but rather just kept looking at her. The frog continued staring into Caroline's eyes even as Caroline picked it up. It even seemed to be a little excited about Caroline's interest - this might sound crazy, but Caroline really felt it.

So Caroline decided right then and there that, despite her father's rule against animals in the house, she needed to take this frog home and keep it as her pet.

And with the rainbow frog sitting happily in her hands, Caroline ran back to her house to figure out how to make a secret home for her new friend.

Chapter 2

Getting back to her house, her small hands still cradling the rainbow frog, Caroline knew that she had two challenges: first, she couldn't just put the frog anywhere, as it needed its own home, with water and food; and second, her father didn't like animals and would definitely not approve of Caroline bringing a frog into their home, no matter how special the frog was.

Her first challenge was the easier one to fix. Caroline snuck in through the side door of her house, opening and closing the door quietly so her father wouldn't hear, and tiptoed upstairs to her room.

Being in Caroline's room was like being inside of a rainbow. Her walls and bed and shelves were covered in shiny colorful things, from the pictures of flowers to the paintings of unicorns to the art she had created herself. Her bookcase was full of her favorite books, like Ramona and Willie Wonka and Guts and a variety of books about girls and unicorns, next to sparkly rocks and shells she had collected over the years. And on top of her bookcase was an old fishbowl, empty and lonely ever since her fish died the previous year.

Caroline stood on a chair to get the fishbowl, only using one hand as her other hand gently cradled the frog. She placed some of her favorite shiny rocks inside the bowl, then added some water from the bathroom sink. She inspected the new home, and then decided to put a small princess character into the fishbowl just to make it look cuter. Once everything looked just the way she wanted, Caroline plopped her new pet frog into its new home.

Peering in at the rainbow frog, Caroline was surprised that it already looked a little different than when she discovered it. "That's strange," she whispered to the rainbow frog, "you look a lot bigger, and even more sparkly somehow."

The frog looked back at Caroline and croaked. Its rainbow-colored back shimmered above the pale green of its body.

Caroline's second challenge was going to be more difficult. She knew that her father didn't want animals in the house, saying they were dirty and just caused problems. Keeping animals in a container like the fishbowl didn't help - he had allowed Caroline's last pet, the fish, but the often dirty water, and Caroline's heartache when the fish died, proved his point.

At the same time, as long as Caroline's new rainbow frog stayed in the fishbowl, she thought she could hide it from her father. This thought made her uncomfortable, feeling like she was lying and hating to hide anything from her father. But she knew in her heart that her new pet was something special, and that she'd figure out a way to convince her father of that. Eventually. Somehow.

So Caroline took the fishbowl with the rainbow frog inside of it and put it on the floor behind her bed. She figured that if she kept her room clean, and made her bed every day, her dad would have no reason to go to the far side of her bed and find her new pet.

Then Caroline wondered if her little sister, Cora, might find the frog and tell on her. But Caroline knew that Cora wouldn't go into her room without Caroline's permission, just like Caroline didn't go into Cora's without her sister's permission, either.

Smiling at her cleverness, Caroline washed the mud from her hands and ran downstairs.

"Oh, Caroline, you're home!" her father said, looking up from his computer, where he was almost always busy writing. "I didn't hear you come in!"

Chapter 3

When she initially brought the rainbow frog home, Caroline assumed that it was fully grown. After all, it was a similar size to all the adult frogs she saw near the creek by her home - the only real difference, or so Caroline thought, was the sparkly rainbow pattern on its back. But to Caroline's surprise, the rainbow frog seemed to grow a little bit every single day. No matter what food she put in its bowl, whether muesli or turkey or seaweed or cucumber, the frog ate all of it, and just kept growing. She never imagined that an animal could grow so quickly!

Soon the rainbow frog barely had room to hop around the fishbowl at all, even after Caroline removed the princess character and some of the rocks. She grew nervous, and hoped it would stop growing.

It didn't.

Caroline really started to get nervous when, after just a couple weeks, the frog became too big to move around the fishbowl at all. Its home, even with all the rocks and decorations removed, was clearly too small. Caroline just kept hoping the frog was done growing.

It wasn't.

Especially since she was a little anxious every day that her father or sister would discover the frog, Caroline often wondered now whether it was time to release the frog back into the wild. But then she would look in at her frog and see how beautiful its shiny rainbow pattern was, becoming ever the more stunning as it grew, and she would see her frog looking back at her with obvious love and affection. And Caroline would decide that, no, she simply couldn't let it go.

But one day Caroline realized that the frog was now almost bigger than the top of the fishbowl, and became more worried than ever. If the frog grew any more, Caroline would never be able to get it out! She had to do something, and she concluded that she didn't have a choice any longer. She had to let the frog go.

So Caroline put the fishbowl, with the rainbow frog still inside of it, in her backpack. The fishbowl was so big that she couldn't zip up her backpack all the way, and it was so heavy with the giant frog inside that she had trouble picking it up, but she finally lifted the half-open backpack over her shoulder and snuck out with it through the side door of her house. With her shoulders slumping under the weight of her backpack, Caroline hiked back to the creek in the forest behind her house - back to where she had found the frog.

"Okay little guy, er, big guy, it's been fun," Caroline said sadly, "but I can't keep you any longer. You're getting too big and I don't know what to do with you, and I also feel so bad not telling Daddy and Cora about you." A tear dripped down her cheek. "It's not right. And I don't think you're happy in such a tiny bowl anyway. So, it's time to say goodbye."

The rainbow frog croaked loudly, louder and deeper than ever before. It almost sounded like a growl to Caroline.

Caroline put the fishbowl on the ground and tipped it to one side, so the open part faced the mud and the frog could easily hop out. The frog tumbled a bit, but once it squirmed upright again, it didn't move.

"C'mon, froggy, it's time to go," Caroline sniveled as she gently tapped the back of the fishbowl.

But the rainbow frog wouldn't move. And even when Caroline tipped the bowl further and shook it a little, the frog stayed inside.

Now Caroline grew frustrated in addition to being sad. "C'mon, froggy, go home!" She reached inside the fishbowl and gently pulled the frog's feet, but the frog scooted backward, staying in the fishbowl like a dog that stubbornly sits while its owner tugs on its leash.

Then Caroline reached her hand behind the frog and tried to pull its whole body out of the fishbowl. But the frog was too big for Caroline to pull it out with her arm also in the opening.

The frog wasn't coming out.

Caroline sat back, into the mud, and cried. "I don't know what to do," she whimpered. "You can't stay in the fishbowl. I can't tell my daddy about you. And now… now I can't get you out." Her cries turned to sobs as she helplessly tried to figure out what to do. The frog seemed to join Caroline's crying with its own long, sad croaks.

"I don't know what to do," Caroline said again. But then, through her tear-blurry eyes, she saw a pile of rocks next to the creek and had an idea. "Or maybe I do," she whispered to herself, standing up and wiping her eyes with the sleeve of her dress.

Caroline walked over to the pile of rocks, picked up the biggest one, and carried it back.

"Please don't get hurt, please don't get hurt," she whispered to the frog as she lifted the rock with two hands and then hit it against the fishbowl. The bowl cracked. She hit it with the rock again, and this time the fishbowl split into two. The rainbow frog hopped forward, getting away from the broken glass. Caroline smiled and picked up the pieces of glass, carefully putting them in her backpack so they wouldn't hurt anyone, or anything.

Caroline looked at the frog, who somehow immediately looked bigger, and shinier, and more wonderful than ever. "Goodbye big guy," she said sadly, but determined. "I'll miss you."

The frog stared deep into Caroline's eyes before Caroline finally turned around and walked away, through the forest, back toward her home.

Chapter 4

When Caroline got back to her house, she stopped and took a few deep breaths before going inside. She knew she would become even more sad when she got to her room and was all alone, no longer having her pet rainbow frog to look at, or feed, or even to worry about. But she also knew that if she walked into the house looking sad, her father would notice, and she didn't want to have to explain things to him - or even worse, didn't want to have to lie to him anymore. So she straightened out her pigtails, dabbed her eyes with the sleeve of her dress (at the same time realizing that her dress was covered in mud, but there was nothing she could do about that yet), and prepared to go inside and act normal.

But right as she was about to turn the doorknob, Caroline heard a loud *"Riiibbit"* behind her. She spun around, and there on the pathway to the side door of her house was her rainbow frog. *"Croooak"*, it said, really seeming like it was trying to talk to Caroline, trying to tell her or even ask her something.

"No!" Caroline said, her mind made up, the hard part over. "Go home!" She turned back around and quickly went inside.

"What do I do now?" Caroline thought to herself as she went up to her room, put down her backpack, and changed into a clean dress. She wanted a distraction from both her guilt and her sadness. She decided to make some soup.

Caroline and her little sister Cora loved to help their father by cooking every now and then, and one of their favorite things to cook was soup, mostly because it was hard to mess up. They had an enormous soup pot, so big that it couldn't fit in the oven but could use two burners on the stove, and they loved to fill it with water, a whole chicken (or two or three!), and all the vegetables they could find.

Caroline pulled the soup pot out of the pantry and began rummaging through the refrigerator for things to put into the soup.

And then she heard the scratching at the door. It sounded like a dog trying to get in, but Caroline's stomach dropped as she realized that it wasn't a dog, but likely a frog, doing the scratching. She tried to ignore it, to continue preparing her soup, but the scratching persisted, over and over again. Every time she thought it was done, that the frog had left, the scratching began again.

Finally, unable to hold herself back any longer, she went and opened the door. As she expected, there was the frog. "No!" she yelled at the big rainbow frog. "You gotta go home!"

But the frog just croaked at her, loudly, and didn't move. It looked up into Caroline's eyes with a look that was full of pleading sadness. The rainbow frog's big bulgy eyes, now with long black eyelashes that Caroline hadn't noticed before, were full of tears, and seemed to beg Caroline to not make it go away, but to let it come inside.

"You think *this* is your home, don't you," Caroline whispered down at the frog. The frog jumped up like a small excited dog (it was in fact now the size of a small dog) and gave a big excited croak as if to say, "Yes!"

Caroline looked back into the kitchen at the giant soup pot, and had an idea. "It's funny," she thought to herself as she knelt down, "My ideas always seem to come only after I've given up." She shrugged and thought, "Anyway, I hope this is a good one!"

She picked up the frog, which was heavier than ever, and, after looking around to make sure no one was coming, carried it into the kitchen. Then she placed it in the soup pot next to some chopped up carrots and onions. The rainbow frog looked up at Caroline with a slightly confused, maybe even nervous look on its froggy little green face.

"Don't worry," Caroline said to the frog with a giggle. "I'm not making frog soup. But this is big enough to be your home, for now at least. At least until I can figure something else out... or until I tell my daddy... or, well, until he finds out. But... but you gotta stop growing."

The rainbow frog hopped happily around the giant soup pot, and then started eating the carrots and onions around it.

Caroline carried the soup pot up to her room and put it down behind her bed. Luckily the pot was just barely shorter than her bed, so it couldn't be seen from the hallway.

Caroline sat on the edge of her mattress and looked down at the frog. She smiled, happy to have her special rainbow frog pet back in her life - even though it hadn't actually been gone very long. The frog's rainbow back was as pretty and shiny as ever, but in addition to the strange (and cute!) new eyelashes, Caroline also noticed small patches of what looked like white fur near the frog's belly.

"Weird," she whispered, half to herself, and half to the rainbow frog. "I've never seen fur on a frog before..." And then Caroline wondered whether the bump on the frog's forehead was also new, or whether she just hadn't noticed it before.

Chapter 5

A couple days later, Caroline was hanging out in her room when she heard her sister Cora yell: "Daddy, have you seen the soup pot?"

Caroline quickly sat up in her bed as her heart jumped into her throat.

"Daddy?" Cora continued yelling. "I want to make some soup, but I can't find the pot anywhere!"

"Soup sounds great, honey," their father finally answered. "But the pot should be in its normal spot. It would be hard to lose." He laughed. "It's big enough to cook you in it, Cora!"

"Not funny daddy," Cora said, as Caroline ran and closed the door to her room.

"Oh no oh no oh no," Caroline whispered to herself. "Why does Cora need to make soup? Why now? Oh no oh no oh no." She ran back to the giant soup pot behind her bed. Looking down at her rainbow frog - whose body was almost half covered in patchy white fur now, whose legs had grown a couple inches and actually lifted its belly off of the bottom of the pot, whose bump on its forehead now looked like a tiny tooth, and who was now the size of a pug - Caroline whispered, "What are we gonna do, little guy? Oh no oh no oh no."

There was a knock on her door. "Carolyn?" her sister said, pronouncing the last syllable of her name, as always, with a short I instead of a long I. Sometimes Caroline found it endearing, kind of her sister's nickname for her, but right now, while she was panicking, it bothered Caroline more than ever.

"You mean Caro*line*, Cora?" Caroline answered, annoyed but also trying to change the subject.

Cora ignored her correction, and through the door asked, "Carolyn have you seen the soup pot?"

"Why would I have seen the soup pot?" Caroline yelled toward the closed door with a nasty tone in her voice. "Why are you making soup, anyway?" she snapped at her sister.

"Aww," Cora whimpered. Walking away from Caroline's room, she mumbled sadly, "I thought you liked soup. Especially when I made it."

Caroline immediately felt bad for snapping at her sister. She did like soup, and did especially enjoy Cora's soup. When Cora made it, the soup always had weird ingredients in it like coconut milk or ginger or beets - ingredients that Caroline was always too afraid to put in her own soup but somehow turned out delicious when Cora used them. Especially for a six-year-old, Cora was quite the chef.

Caroline became overwhelmed by guilt. She felt in her stomach how much she hated keeping any secrets from her family. So she ran to her door, opened it a tiny bit, and peeked out.

"Psst. Cora," Caroline whispered as loudly as she could. "Cora! Come here."

Sensing a good secret, Cora quickly turned around, smiled at Caroline, and skipped back toward her room.

"Come in," Caroline said to Cora, opening the door just wide enough to let her in. "But be quiet, kay?"

"Mmhmm!" Cora said, quickly nodding, her eyes wide with excitement. She slid her body past Caroline's door like she was on a secret mission.

"But you have to keep a secret," Caroline said, closing the door behind her. "Can you do that, Cora?"

"Hey what's that?" Cora said before answering her sister, pointing behind Caroline's bed. "Hey, that's the soup pot!"

"Shhh!"

"What's it doing behind your bed?" Cora walked toward the pot. "Are you already making soup? Why in your room?

That's weird... Ahhhh!" Cora screamed when she saw what was inside the pot.

"Quiet!" Caroline growled as quietly as she could while jumping and waving her arms at Cora. The rainbow frog croaked, as if echoing Caroline's plea.

"What kind of soup are you making?" Cora said, not lowering her voice at all, looking up at Caroline with a disgusted look on her face. The frog croaked deeply. Looking back down at the frog, Cora squealed in horror. "What *is* that thing? It does *not* look yummy."

Caroline put her arms on Cora's shoulders. "You need to be quiet or you'll get us in trouble."

"Us?" Cora asked, looking up in shock at her big sister.

"Well, yeah. I mean, it can be your pet too?"

"A pet?" Cora asked, calmer, suddenly very interested. "But, what is it?"

"It's a frog," Caroline said, as if it was obvious.

"That..." Cora said, pointing, "That is not a frog."

Caroline looked down into the pot and realized, finally, that Cora was right: her pet was not a frog. With the extended legs and soft white fur and elongated body and little neck, the rainbow frog was certainly not a frog anymore.

"Hm. It was a frog," Caroline said. "A really pretty rainbow frog."

"I've never heard of a rainbow frog before," Cora said, looking the creature over. "And really, it looks more like a sick dog, ew. But, its back sure is colorful and shiny."

Cora smiled as the frog looked up lovingly into her eyes and batted its long eyelashes.

"Hi little guy," Cora whispered. Then, looking back at Caroline she asked, "What's her name?"

"Um, rainbow frog?"

Cora giggled. "You're always terrible at naming things. Hello… rainbow frog."

"And why do you think it's a girl, anyway?" Caroline asked Cora, realizing that she had only thought of the frog as an "it" up to that point.

"Look at her beautiful eyelashes. Of course it's a girl!"

The frog hopped around the pot in approval, though it was a pretty awkward hop now that its legs were getting straighter and its body was off the ground.

Cora smiled at the frog, but then said to Caroline, "You know daddy is never going to let you keep her, though, right?"

Caroline grimaced. "I know. But for now, can we keep it a secret?"

"Daddy doesn't like secrets."

"I know, Cora, I know. And neither do I. But, can we, maybe just a little while longer? Please?"

Chapter 6

Cora did keep the secret, the biggest secret of her life, and by far the biggest shared between the two sisters. "I decided not to make soup after all," Cora told her father when he later asked about the pot, and the soup.

But the "rainbow frog" (as they kept calling her, for a while, as Caroline couldn't come up with any alternatives), the "rainbow frog" continued to grow, and to change. Soon about the size of a small retriever, her legs had grown longer, and became hard around her feet. Her head grew bigger and extended further from her body as her new neck grew longer. Her shiny white hair now covered nearly her whole body, to the point that Caroline and Cora couldn't see her green skin anymore (assuming her skin was still green), and they had to look hard to see the shimmering rainbow skin on her back. And, finally, the little tooth on the "frog's" head kept growing longer and was in fact now a small white horn, over an inch long, pointed, and the soft shiny texture of a pearl.

The "rainbow frog" still slept in the soup pot, but she was now dry enough not to need any water to sit in, which also meant she no longer made messes when she was out of the pot. This allowed Caroline to play with her on the floor of her room and on her bed, and she let Cora do the same (part of the deal to make sure Cora didn't tell their father anything).

Cora also helped feed the "frog" since there was only so much food Caroline could save from her lunch or sneak from the kitchen without their father noticing. And to both of their relief, it seemed like despite how much she ate and drank, the "rainbow frog" never had to pee or poop - that would have made things especially tricky, of course.

While all three were hanging out together in Caroline's room one afternoon, Cora was inspecting all these changes in the "frog" while stroking its smooth little white horn. Then she looked up at her sister and said, "Carolyn, I'm pretty sure she's a unicorn."

Caroline was shocked. "That's silly, Cora. Unicorns aren't real."

"Then what do you think it is? She's *definitely* not a frog."

Caroline sighed. "Hmmm… I don't know." She thought about it. "I guess you're right. But, a unicorn?"

"She does have the one horn," Cora said, shrugging her shoulders. "And what else has one horn? She looks way more like a horse than a rhino. And she's definitely not a narwhal." Cora pet the smooth white fur. "And either way, I think it's silly to keep calling her 'rainbow frog', which means she doesn't even have a name anymore. And that's sad."

Caroline smirked, and imagined: what if it was a unicorn? As she watched Cora pet the horn, she realized that there would really be no harm in pretending. She enjoyed pretending, and did love unicorn games. And then she thought: if, or rather when, their father found out about their secret pet, maybe saying it was a unicorn would give them a better chance of keeping her.

So Caroline said: "Okay, Cora. Her name is now, 'Euni'. Euni the unicorn."

Cora giggled. "That's a silly name, Carolyn. Uni like U-N-I? Too easy!"

"No," Caroline protested. "Like the real name Euni. E-U-N-I."

Cora shrugged. "I guess that's a little better. And 'Euni' is *definitely* better than 'Rainbow Frog'." Cora looked into the animal's big kind eyes and said, "Hello, Euni."

Both Cora and Caroline thought they saw Euni smile at her new name.

Part 2: Euni Speaks

Chapter 7

A few weeks later, and after a long day at school (with most of the day spent thinking about Euni, as usual), Caroline returned home to find the door to her bedroom open. She panicked, thinking her father must have gone into her room, and if he had there was no way he wouldn't have seen Euni. Looking around her bedroom, Euni was nowhere to be found. With her heart in her throat, Caroline started running around the house in search of her pet unicorn.

Fearing the worst, she first went to her father's office and peeked inside. He heard his door creak open, and, looking up from his writing, smiled and said, "Welcome home Caroline! How was your day?"

"Good!" Caroline said, relieved that her father obviously hadn't found Euni, but also still panicked as to where she could be. Next Caroline ran to Cora's bedroom, but her sister wasn't home yet, and there was no sign of Euni inside. Then Caroline heard a *click click* sound coming from the kitchen.

Running toward the kitchen, Caroline heard her father yell from his office, "Caroline! How many times have I told you sweetie, no tap shoes in the house! It dents the floors!"

Click click click. And when Caroline, following the sound, made it to the kitchen, there was Euni. Now the size of a large dog, Euni was walking around and sticking her nose into cupboards, while her small hooves made a little *click* sound with every step.

Caroline grabbed Euni by the neck and pulled her toward the stairs. "Euni!" she whispered sternly. "You're gonna get us in trouble!" Together they walked up the stairs, which were fortunately carpeted so the clicking noises stopped. "Do you want to be able to stay here or not? If my daddy sees you…"

Caroline led Euni back into her room and quickly closed the door behind them. "If you're hungry, I'll get you more food, I'll figure something out, but Euni, you can't leave my room!"

"*Mina. Ama Lapa*," Euni said, sounding almost like a horse's bray, but more delicate, and actually sounding like words. Nonsense words, sure, but words nonetheless.

"Wha?" Caroline said, her jaw dropping in shock at Euni's new, strange sounds. She hadn't heard Euni make any sort of sounds since she had stopped croaking weeks before. "Are those…words? Euni, did you just…"

"*Ama Lapa*," Euni said again. "*Ama Lapa, Koo.*"

"What does that mean?" Caroline asked, still in shock. "What are you trying to say to me, Euni?"

Euni shook her head quickly, seeming frustrated. Her head was now the size and shape of a small pony, a big head for a still smallish body (at least as far as ponies are concerned). Meanwhile her horn had grown so big that Caroline's fist couldn't cover it completely - when Caroline held Euni's horn, as she often did because it felt good and even magical somehow, the pearly white tip would stick out above Caroline's hand. Euni waved this horn around as she said: "*Euneeee, Ama Lapa!*"

Caroline's eyes opened wide in surprise. "Euni? You know your name, Euni?"

"*Euneee,*" Euni brayed gently. Followed by, "*Ama Lapaaa.*"

"*Lapa?*" Caroline said, trying to figure out what Euni was saying.

Euni opened and closed her mouth, almost like she was chewing gum.

Caroline thought of what Euni had been doing in the kitchen and realized, "Euni! Are you hungry? *Lapa,* hungry?"

Euni looked at Caroline curiously. Caroline pretended to take a bite from an apple and chew, and then asked, "*Lapa?*"

Euni nodded vigorously. "*Lapa!*"

"*Lapa* means hungry!" Caroline said, excited. She rummaged through her backpack and found what was left of her lunch. She began feeding Euni the few crackers, slices of apple, and kale chips she had left over.

Caroline smiled widely, still amazed. "Euni *Lapa*, Euni hungry."

Euni tilted her big head, then said, "*Ni Euni Lapa! Euni Ama Lapa.*"

"*Ama Lapa,*" Caroline whispered, trying hard to figure out the difference. Then it struck her: "Euni, does *Lapa* mean food?" She pointed at a slice of apple.

Euni seemed to smile.

"So *Ama Lapa* must mean you want food. *Ama* is want, *Lapa* is food?"

Euni nodded her big head vigorously and brayed, "*Eeee.*"

Caroline smiled, incredibly excited now. "*Eee* must mean yes. And a minute ago, you said *Ni* Euni *Lapa*… so *Ni*, *Ni* must mean No, or Not." Then Caroline giggled, realizing what she had said to Euni before. "Of course Euni isn't food! *Ni Euni Lapa*. Euni wants food, Euni *Ama Lapa*!"

Euni grinned widely, and enthusiastically responded, "*Eeee!*"

"And what was the other thing you said, Euni? Was it, *Mina?*"

Euni looked down at the ground, and repeated, "*Minaaa.*"

"And when you said *Mina*," Caroline considered out loud, "it was after I got mad at you. Could *Mina* mean, Sorry?"

Euni nodded her big head and horn. "*Eee.*"

Caroline gave Euni a huge hug around her strong thick neck.

Caroline was amazed and excited. She also realized that even while she was struggling to understand Euni, Euni seemed to already understand many of Caroline's words. She wondered if Euni had been learning English by listening to Caroline and Cora speak, even if she wasn't able to speak it herself.

Considering this, Caroline placed one hand on Euni's shoulder and one hand over her own heart, and asked, "Euni, do you know my name?"

Euni nodded again. "*Carolinnn*".

A tear of joy dripped down Caroline's cheek.

"Close enough," Caroline whispered to Euni. Then she smiled as she realized that Euni must have learned her name through Cora's use of it - something Caroline suddenly found sweeter and more endearing than ever, even if it wasn't accurate.

Chapter 8

Caroline became eager to understand Euni's strange language, and the more words Caroline learned, the more Euni spoke to Caroline.

"Euni Ama Zapaku Dattu," Euni said to Caroline one day, while lying on the floor next to Caroline's bed. By now the giant soup pot was back in the cupboard in the kitchen

where it belonged - Euni had long outgrown it, her body now the size of a small pony.

Caroline learned one word at a time, and while she kept a journal to keep track of Uni's words, she rarely forgot them. Caroline even began the understand much of what Euni said as she spoke. So when Euni said, *"Euni Ama Zapaku Dattu,"* Caroline actually heard Euni say "I want *Zapaku Dattu.*"

And then, each time, the challenge was to figure out what those mysterious Euni words meant. Fortunately, Euni was also getting better at teaching Caroline her language, while and understanding more and more of Caroline's English words.

Euni stood up and, using her big muzzle, pushed Caroline's mattress. *"Dattu,"* Euni said, nudging. *"Dattoooo."*

"Okay," Caroline said. *"Dattu.* Bed."

"Eee," Euni said, which Caroline now heard as "Yes."

Caroline was continually amazed at Euni's ability to understand her words, but she was also confused by where Euni's language came from, since Euni couldn't have learned it from anyone or anything else. It was like a unicorn language that Euni seemed to instinctively know to speak — a language that Euni magically knew, even.

This mysterious origin of Euni's language made Caroline even more eager to learn it. Caroline pulled out the journal she kept near her bed and added to her vocabulary list: *Dattu = Bed*.

"So what's *Zapaku*?" she asked.

Euni walked over to Caroline's closet and pushed aside some dresses. Then, carefully using her thick pink lips, Euni tugged on a fuzzy pink sweater. "*Zapaku!*" Euni said.

"Pink?" Caroline asked. "You want a pink bed?"

"*Ni! Ni Euni Ama Rishi Dattu,*" Euni said, or as Caroline now understood: "No! I don't want a *Rishi* bed."

Caroline quickly wrote down *Rishi = Pink*.

Euni rubbed her muzzle against the fuzzy pink sweater, and again said, "*Zapaku!*"

"Oh!" Caroline exclaimed. "*Zapaku* means furry, or soft?"

"*Eee!*" Euni said.

Caroline looked down at the floor next to her bed, at the firm, thin pink rug covering the cold hardwood. She shook

44

her head, disappointed in herself. "Of course you want a soft bed, Euni. What was I thinking, that you'd be okay sleeping on the floor like that?" She thought about her options. "You're too big to sleep with me… almost too big to even hide anywhere in my room anymore… I'm gonna have to think about this one."

Suddenly there was a knock at Caroline's door. Caroline jumped in surprise.

"Sweetie?" her dad said from the other side.

Caroline got up from her bed while waving her arms at Euni. "Quick, Euni, get down, hide," she whispered.

Euni got as low as she could on the floor behind Caroline's bed.

Caroline ran to the door and opened it a few inches. "Yes daddy?" she said, sweetly.

Her father glanced over Caroline's head and into her bedroom before asking, "Who are you talking to in there?"

"Talking to?"

"Yeah," he said, looking confused. "I heard you talking… like you were, uh, having a conversation with someone."

"Um… no," she replied.

"No?" he asked, while looking around her room some more. "No one else is in here?"

"Of course not daddy!" she said, trying hard to sound normal.

He looked back down at Caroline. "Is everything okay?" he asked her.

"Of course!" Caroline said. "I… I was just playing with my dolls, that's all."

"Okay…" her father said. "Well, anyway, I gotta run an errand, but I'll be back soon. If your sister gets home before me, keep an eye on her, kay? Play a game with her or something?"

"Sure daddy!" Caroline said. "I will, no problem!"

Her father left and Caroline closed her door, relieved. As he walked down the hallway, her father wondered where all the dolls were that Caroline said she had been playing with – and also, why she would be so enthusiastic all of the sudden about looking after Cora.

"Caroline sure has been acting weird," he whispered to himself. "I hope she's doing okay."

Chapter 9

Caroline soon developed a decent understanding of Euni's day-to-day language. This mostly consisted of small requests, such as *"Yeestee Euni Oomoo Koo"* ("Scratch my ears please"), or *"Euni Ama Lapa"* (when she was hungry), but also became more detailed, such as *"Euni Ama Biskik A Zapaku Leemee"* ("I want kale and soft peaches"). Cora also picked up some words and phrases here and there, though she was much more content to just cuddle and talk at Euni, while letting Caroline do the real work.

But as this was going on, Euni just kept growing. Euni was now the size of a small horse, and too big to effectively hide behind Caroline's bed anymore - even when Euni tried her absolute best, her horn and tops of her shoulders would protrude above the bed. This led to Caroline always keeping her door closed, and living in fear of the day that her father would come into her room and discover her secret. So Caroline was back in the predicament of figuring out a real plan for her pet.

By now, Euni was clearly a unicorn. Along with beautiful sparkling white hair and a rainbow-colored mane (all that was left of the rainbow frog's colorful back), Euni had that glorious single horn coming out of her forehead. The horn felt like a tooth to Caroline and Cora, but glimmered like a polished pearl, and had a swirl pattern like that of a twisted lollipop. Like a pearl it was a radiant white color, but when the sun shone in through Caroline's window and struck the horn just right, it would erupt in a rainbow – similar to how when the sun shines on a soap bubble, a small rainbow ripples on its surface.

But Caroline was also now full of guilt toward Euni, feeling truly bad for her unicorn. Euni was an animal, drawn to the outdoors, and spent most of her alone time staring out of Caroline's window (fortunately there were just trees on the other side of the window, and no people to look in!). Euni also often had trouble getting comfortable, despite the furry blanket Caroline bought for her using all the money she had collected through birthday gifts from grandparents and payments from the tooth fairy. And Euni's legs were so long that she could only take three or four steps forward in Caroline's room before having to turn around again.

But, despite knowing she had to do something, Caroline simply didn't know what to do. Euni was past the point of being able to just be set free into the woods. Or so Caroline thought.

Therefore it should have come as no surprise when one day Euni said to Caroline, "*Euni Ema Ghee Atata.*" But these were words Caroline hadn't heard before, so the two began

49

their normal routine of charades, where Euni would teach Caroline what each word meant.

Euni started with "*Atata*", sticking her muzzle against the window until Caroline understood "Outside". Next, Caroline figured out that "*Ghee*" meant "Go."

"Okay. So, Euni, you... *Ema*... go outside..." Caroline said, cringing.

Then Euni got excited, loudly braying "*Euni Ema Dalini, Ah Daluni.*" She trotted (three steps) back and forth in Caroline's room, and then started happily throwing pillows and stuffed animals into the air - making quite a noisy mess until Caroline figured out that "*Dalini Ah Daluni*" meant "Run and Play."

"But Euni," Caroline said, "What's *Ema*? I know *Ama* means want, but is *Ema* different?"

At this Euni turned to Caroline, her big horse face inches from Caroline's own. "*Ama*," Euni said, softly, looking down at the ground between them. "*Euni Ama,*" she said again, gently. Then Euni looked directly into Caroline's eyes, staring with her big hazel eyes through thick black eyelashes intently into Caroline's own brown eyes, and loudly brayed, "*Eema!*" It was so loud it made Caroline jump in surprise. And still staring into Caroline's eyes, Euni again yelled (as far as she could yell), "*Euni Eeeema!*"

"I get it," Caroline said. "*Ama* means want, *Ema* means need."

"*Eee!*" Euni said loudly, which of course Caroline heard as "Yes". "*Euni Ema Ghee Atata, Euni Ema Dalini Ah Daluni, Atata,*" Euni yelled. Which Caroline finally understood as "I need to go outside! I need to run and play, outside!"

And Caroline grimaced, unsure of what to do, or how to respond.

Suddenly the door to Caroline's bedroom opened, making Caroline spin around in total surprise. As she turned toward her door Caroline assumed it was Cora, and was ready to get mad at her for not knocking first.

"Caroline!" her father said. "What is going on in here?"

Caroline just watched her father as he stepped into her room; watched him as he initially looked to her to answer his question; watched him as he then looked over at Euni.

His jaw dropped.

Chapter 10

Caroline and her father sat across from one another at their dining room table. "Caroline, you know the rule against animals in our house," he said. His voice was full of anger and disappointment - Caroline wasn't sure which one more so, but each emotion stung in its own way.

Cora stood in the corner of the dining room, silently watching and listening. And while Caroline's father was facing the girls, facing what was the wrong direction, Caroline and Cora could see Euni through the kitchen window. Euni had been immediately ushered outside after being discovered by Cora and Caroline's father, and now the girls tried their best to not to look at her as she watched the three of them through the window.

"I know," Caroline said. "But Daddy…"

"No 'but Daddy!' Not only is this an animal in the house Caroline, but a giant animal, a wild animal… A freaking horse!"

"She's not a…"

"Stop! Just listen to me, Caroline! A horse, inside our house! In your room! Do you know how dirty horses are? And how dangerous? One kick, Caroline, one kick, and… and I don't even want to imagine!"

"But Daddy…"

"And did you ever stop and think about the horse itself? You think it's happy in your room? It's a wild animal, it wants to run free! It must have been miserable up there! I feel like I just saved it!"

Caroline looked down at the table between her and her father as her tears silently began falling. She knew he was right. She had known it for days, if not weeks. Horse or not, she knew that keeping such a large animal in her room was wrong, inhumane even, and must have been making Euni miserable - even if it was only that day that Euni said she needed the outdoors.

"But Caroline, let me tell you," her father said, quieter now, less angry, more sad, "the thing I'm most disappointed about is that you didn't tell me. You knew the rule, knew how I felt, and you decided not to tell me, which is basically the same thing as lying to me. It breaks my heart that you would do that, Caroline."

At this, Caroline started sobbing, loudly. But to her surprise, both this moment and the sobbing were each a relief. She had been keeping this secret for so long, since that very first day with the little rainbow frog from the creek - had been lying to her father for so long - that it felt so good to not have to keep her secret anymore.

So Caroline cried and cried, feeling so sad, so regretful, but also so relieved that she didn't have to lie to her father anymore.

"I'm sorry, Daddy," she whimpered. "I'm so sorry."

"Me too, sweetie," he whispered.

Caroline's father moved his chair next to hers and gently rubbed her back in silence while she cried. He spent the time thinking about how strange Caroline had been acting for weeks, maybe even months, and how confused he had been about what to do. He finally asked her, "How long has this been going on, sweetie?"

Caroline didn't look up, didn't respond. So he turned to Cora, still standing quietly in the corner: "Cora, did you know about the horse, too?"

Cora's eyes widened, like she thought she had been invisible up until that moment. And instead of answering, she ran out of the dining room toward the direction of her bedroom. Her father laughed a little, through his nose, which made Caroline look up.

Then he sighed, deeply. "I guess it doesn't matter, now," he said. "A lie is a lie. And it must have been eating you up inside, given the Caroline I know and love."

He was right. She realized only then the suffering that the secrets and lies were causing her, realized the weight they put on her, every day.

"Will you tell me why, at least?" he asked her. "Why you didn't tell me? Why it was that important to torture yourself over, especially because you had to know I'd find out eventually." Then he laughed, through his nose, again. "That I'd smell the horse poop, eventually."

A smile crept over Caroline's lips, but quickly retreated. "Because I knew you wouldn't understand, daddy. And… and because I couldn't let her go."

"Wouldn't understand what? You wanting a horse?"

"Not a horse."

"I know it's fun to pretend," he said, grimacing. "But do you really think the horse likes having a big horn stuck on its head? I mean, how'd you even get it to stay on like that? It can't be comfortable. In fact…"

"It's not pretend," Caroline interrupted.

"Sweetie, c'mon. What are you saying?"

"I'm saying she's a unicorn. A real live unicorn. And that... that I couldn't let her go. And... and I'm pretty sure, actually, that she doesn't *want* to go."

"Honey," he said, gently touching her wet cheek. "You know unicorns aren't real. I love your imagination, it's one of my favorite things about you, but don't you think this is going too far?"

"I told you you wouldn't understand," she said.

Her father sat back in his chair and considered. "Okay," he finally said. "Let's pretend it's a unicorn."

"She *is* a unicorn. And her name is Eumi."

"Okay, she's a unicorn. Still, even if they existed, unicorns would be wild animals, just like horses. And they'd want to run free, not be stuck in a small bedroom. So now that it's back, er, she's back outside, I'm sure she's long gone, back to her family even." He pictured it, then smiled. "And they're probably busy trying to get that silly horn off her head."

"Daddy! It's not silly, it's a real horn. And anyway, she wants to stay with me, I know it!"

57

Her father sighed, losing patience. "How do you know," he asked.

"Look over there," Caroline said, and pointed past him toward the kitchen window.

Her father turned in his seat, and sure enough, Euni's muzzle was pressed right up against the window. Noticing the attention, Euni brayed, *"Euni Ama Carolynnn. Euni Ni Ama Ghee."*

"What the…" Caroline's father sputtered. "And what are those noises?"

"She said she wants me. And that she doesn't want to go."

"Caroline, that's enough." Her father said, slapping his hand on the table. "I've had enough. First the animal, then the lying, and now this. I thought you were sorry, but you're clearly not." He stood up. "I've had enough, and it's time to end this." He pulled out his phone. "I'm calling animal control. They'll come and deal with it."

"No!" Caroline screamed. "No daddy, I'll tell her to leave! Just, just don't!"

"Tell her?" he said, getting angrier. "Caroline, this is ridiculous!" He took a deep breath. "But fine, fine, you have 30 seconds to get that… thing… far away from here, or else I'm calling. 30 seconds."

Caroline jumped up from the table, hurried outside through the side door, and ran to Euni. Caroline's father noticed that Euni, whatever she was, was obviously excited to see Caroline coming toward her.

Her father watched through the kitchen window as Caroline spoke to Euni; watched as the animal's excitement waned, then went away completely; watched as his daughter and her wild pet walked in opposite directions. The "horse" ambled away from the house and into the woods, while his daughter ran back into the house and directly up to her room, where her father could hear her sobbing uncontrollably.

Chapter 11

Often in life, time heals wounds better than anything else possibly could.

This is especially the case in a world where magic is very rare.

So as the days and weeks crept by, so incredibly slowly at first, Caroline began hurting less and less from the absence of Euni in her life, and started getting back to the normal life of an nine-year-old girl.

In the morning she'd have breakfast with her father and sister. Usually it was oatmeal along with eggs that she would cook herself, though sometimes Cora would prepare the oatmeal the night before, and sometimes her father would cook up a special treat like french toast or waffles. Then Caroline would go off to school, where she'd learn about grammar and history and multiplication and other such things that, in her sadness, seemed meaningless. After school she'd usually have an activity, like piano lessons or Hebrew school or kung fu or sewing, and after that she'd walk home and help her father cook dinner. Every night Caroline, Cora, and their father ate dinner together, after which Caroline would take a shower while Cora took a bath. Before bedtime the girls would call their mother, who lived in Australia, to wish her good morning while she wished them goodnight. Then it was bedtime, time first for a ridiculous made-up story from their father before getting a good night's sleep, all in preparation to do it all over again the following day.

On the weekends they would often go to temple on Saturdays, and spend the rest of the time doing fun activities as a family, whether it be going to the farmers' market, or going on a hike in the woods behind their house, or having playdates with other families, or visiting grandparents in the city (though Caroline didn't really like the city - even though she loved seeing her grandparents, she always missed the trees, animals, and empty spaces near her home).

It was one such weekend, on a Saturday afternoon, that Caroline and Cora were running around behind their house, playing a pretend game of monsters and princesses.

"Rawrrr!" Cora yelled, chasing Caroline. "I'm going to get you, princess! You can't escape now!"

Caroline giggled and ran through the woods away from Cora. But Cora was quick, and was catching up, so Caroline decided to start climbing a tree whose branches looked perfect.

"Luckily you can't climb trees, you scary monster!" Caroline yelled, climbing as fast as she could.

Cora looked up at the climbing Caroline and roared again. "I can't climb," she growled, "but I'm ginormous, so

I'm still gonna reach up and get you if you don't hurry!"
Cora reached her arms in the air and waved them like she
imagined a scary monster would. "Rawrrr!"

Caroline laughed. "I better go higher!" she yelled, and
continued to climb and climb, branch upon branch like a
giant ladder, going higher and higher in the tree.

"Rawrr!"

Suddenly a branch snapped beneath Caroline's
scrambling foot, making her slip. She tried to hold on with
only her hands, but the branch she grasped onto also
snapped under the sudden weight.

Caroline screamed as she fell from the tree. She tumbled
through the air, bending and breaking all the branches
beneath her before finally landing on her side, right next to
Cora.

"Carolyn!" Cora gasped, bending down to her sister.
"Carolyn, are you okay?"

Caroline was quiet for a moment before looking up at
Cora. Then she went to sit up, and she screamed, louder
than Cora had ever heard, louder than Caroline had ever
screamed before.

Caroline looked down at her right forearm. Seeing that it was slightly bent halfway between her wrist and her elbow, she screamed again.

Cora looked down at her big sister's arm, shrieked in horror, and panicked. Seeing Caroline's broken arm, Cora wanted to throw up, and wanted to run away - but Cora also knew that she had to be brave, as her sister needed her help.

"Can you stand up?" she asked Caroline. Looking around for help, all Cora saw was empty woods.

Fortunately, with Cora's help Caroline was able to stand up, and had no problem walking. So with Cora leading the way for her crying sister, they made their way back to their home without any more challenges.

Their father, who also looked like he wanted to vomit at the sight of his daughter's broken arm, kept calm and loaded the girls into the car and drove to the hospital. He tried the best he could to hide his silent tears.

Caroline needed surgery to put her bones (her radius and ulna bones) back into the right spots. After surgery, in order to keep the bones in the right place while they healed, Caroline got a thick pink cast that covered her arm all the way from the palm of her hand to her elbow. The doctor explained to her that it was a bad break, and could take up to three months to heal, but that he would do another x-ray in 6 weeks to check on her progress. So even after the surgery was over and the cast was on, Caroline did a lot of crying.

The day after getting home from the hospital, Caroline and Cora sat in their backyard, on the edge of the nearby woods, while Cora begged Caroline to play with her. "Your legs are fine," Cora told her big sister. "We can still play!"

"I don't want to," Caroline said, looking down at her cast, feeling sorry for herself. "Just, leave me alone for a while, okay? Go play by yourself?"

Cora frowned, feeling bad for her sister. "I wish I got hurt instead of you," she said to Caroline.

"Don't say that," Caroline said. "You have no idea how much it hurt. I'm glad it was me."

The two sat quietly together for a few more minutes before Cora had an idea. She perked up and said, "Okay, I'm gonna go to the creek. Maybe I'll find an animal for you to play with?"

This made Caroline even more sad, bringing back memories of the rainbow frog, and of Euni - of the unicorn friend she had loved, and lost. But she just said "Okay, fine, go." And off Cora went, while Caroline sat alone and sulked.

A few minutes later, sitting all alone, crying softly while staring at her cast, watching her tears soak the cast while she pictured how gross her arm had looked, Caroline heard a rustling noise from the forest.

"Cora?" she said. The rustling grew louder. Caroline yelled into the woods now: "Cora, is that you?"

But from between the trees, out came Euni. She looked more beautiful than ever, definitely bigger than the last time Caroline had seen her, and with her rainbow mane more full and flowing than ever before.

"Euni!" Caroline squealed, jumping up and running to her friend. But Euni didn't get excited. Instead she just stared sadly at the cast on Caroline's arm, stared with big teary eyes even while Caroline hugged her using her one good arm.

Chapter 12

"*Koo Deepee Carolinn,*" Euni brayed. Caroline was familiar enough with each of the words to understand: "Please sit, Caroline."

Caroline did as she was told. She was no longer feeling sorry for herself and her broken arm, but she was suddenly nervous about what Euni was going to say, or do. Caroline had never seen her beloved Euni acting so seriously.

Euni knelt to one knee in front of Caroline, and then lowered her giant, sparkling white head. As she tipped her head down, Euni's mane tumbled forward, and Caroline was amazed to see what looked like a real rainbow appear between the unicorn's long, dangling hairs.

Euni placed her long, glistening, pearl-colored horn on Caroline's cast.

Both Euni and Caroline grew still, and perfectly silent. After a few moments the spiral unicorn horn began to glow slightly, as if a light was slowly turning on from within. And then Caroline felt a warmth in her arm, and the warmth increased and expanded until its tingling heat grew uncomfortable - but Caroline was too mesmerized, and too trusting, to move.

Just before the heat grew unbearable to Caroline the sensation became soothing, and soon after that, the light in Euni's horn disappeared. Only then did Euni lift her head to look at Caroline.

Euni's pleasant, loving look was back in her eyes, replacing all signs of the concern she had a minute earlier.

"*Carolyn Ni Zilchi,*" Euni said to Caroline.

Caroline responded, "*Zilchi?* I don't know *Zilchi.* But, Euni, are you saying, somehow… Could you be saying, that… that I'm not broken anymore? That my arm is healed?"

Euni smiled widely. "*Eeee,*" she brayed.

"I, I…" Caroline stumbled over her words. "I need to tell my daddy."

Euni smiled again, and then simply said, "*Ee.*"

Caroline ran inside and interrupted her father's typing to tell him about Euni and her arm. She knew interrupting him would frustrate him, and she also knew he would be upset about hearing of Euni again, but she just had to tell him what happened. She had to prove to him, immediately, that Euni was special.

"Caroline, I warned you about playing with that wild animal!" her father said, very annoyed, after listening to most of her story.

"Please, daddy, please, can we just ask the doctor to take another look? Just a quick look!" Caroline was almost in tears, a mixture of fear and excitement and frustration and wonder.

"You realize how crazy this sounds, don't you? To me? And then how crazy this would sound to the doctor?"

"Yes, Daddy, I know, but please, please trust me on this, and if I'm wrong, you'll never hear anything about Euni ever again." Caroline meant it, too. If that moment with Euni, and Euni's horn, had done nothing to Caroline's arm, Caroline decided she would do everything she could to stop even thinking of her old friend and pet anymore. "I promise," she said.

At the same time, she trusted Euni so much, and had felt so much in that magical moment with her, that Caroline wasn't actually worried about following through on her promise.

Her father sighed, considering. He thought the whole thing was crazy, and that his daughter's stories were now completely out of hand - but he also really wanted to trust her. He wanted her to always feel like she could be honest with him. He wanted her to always know he was there for her, no matter what.

Suddenly Cora came crashing through the door to their father's office, using her body to open it since her two hands were busy cradling something in front of her. She ran into the room, brown water dripping from her carefully cupped hands onto the hardwood floor.

"Carolyn, Carolyn, look what I found to cheer you up!" Cora yelled.

Caroline and her father looked over at her, and then down into her muddy hands.

"It's a frog!" Cora exclaimed. "From the creek!" She looked up at her big sister with a goofy smile on her face, and as she did so a little green frog leapt out of her hands. It plopped onto the floor, spattering mud all around it.

"Cora!" her father gasped, standing up from behind his desk.

"That's a normal frog," Caroline told her sister, disappointed. "And a really messy one."

"I know," Cora said. "But... but I just wanted to cheer you up. With... something." Cora looked from the frog, who jumped again and made another little muddy plop, back up to her big sister, and then said, "But it looks like you're already cheered up! Guess I'm too late?"

Caroline smiled at her little sister. "Euni fixed my arm," she said.

"Amazing!" Cora yelled. "I knew she was magical!" In her excitement she dropped the rest of the muddy water from her hands onto the office floor.

"But daddy doesn't believe me. Says it's impossible."

"It is impossible!" Cora squealed to their father. "It's unicorn magic!"

"Fine, Caroline," their father grumbled. "I'll call the doctor."

"Thank you daddy!" Caroline jumped up and down. "Thank you thank you thank you!" She ran behind his desk and gave him a hug, and accidentally hit the back of his head with her big pink cast as she did so. "Oops, sorry sorry daddy!"

But he laughed. "It's okay," he said. And then scratching his head where her cast had hit him he said, "But now I need to figure out a way to convince the doctor to take another look. Without seeming too crazy myself."

Caroline hugged him again, harder this time, and more careful with her cast.

"But for now, I need both of you to clean up this muddy mess! And Cora, get that frog out of this house!"

Chapter 13

"You know this is crazy," the doctor told the three of them, but mostly directed at Caroline's father. He sounded very annoyed. "Absolutely insane. We did the surgery just last week, and now you want another x-ray. Nuts, I tell you."

"I know, I know," Caroline's father said. "I told Caroline the same thing. But she has this notion in her head, and I just need your help dispelling it. Just show her that her arm hasn't changed, and we'll be out of your hair."

The bald doctor rubbed his head before replying. "I'm not surprised that the little girls have made up some stories to feel better about the broken arm. It was a nasty break, after all," the doctor said. "But I expect more out of you, as their father, to dispel these notions yourself."

Caroline and Cora's father sighed as his girls anxiously looked on. He didn't feel like justifying his parenting to the doctor, didn't feel like explaining how important it was to him for his daughters to know they could rely on him, no matter how crazy the topic seemed to others. "I understand doctor," he said instead, "but please, just do this quickly, and…"

"You know there's other patients waiting, right? That time spent on *this* is time taken from other patients. Patients who aren't full of crazy stories, and actually *need* help!"

"I understand, doctor," their father said. "But at the same time, the more time you spend arguing, the more time you're taking away from those patients, right? Can we please just do the x-ray?"

"And then there's Misha's, the radiologist's, time to do the x-ray, and then the time to read it, all just to confirm what we already know! I could just show you the x-ray from last week…"

"Doctor," Caroline's father interrupted, more sternly now. "For me, please, can we just get this over with?"

The doctor glared at Caroline's father. Then he looked down at Caroline, then to her cast, and then back up at her father. The doctor was clearly unhappy, his lips pursed, and did nothing to hide it. "Hm," he grunted. "Fine. But you'll have to pay for the x-ray yourself, insurance won't cover it. But if that's acceptable, if you'll pay, then fine. Let's get this over with."

"Done," her father said, and then echoed the doctor: "Let's get this over with."

So Caroline and her father went to the x-ray room in the far back of the doctor's office, while Cora returned to the waiting room to play with some toys. In the x-ray room Caroline changed into a gown while the doctor whispered to the radiologist, an extremely tall and uncomfortably skinny man with messy wild black hair and a long, scraggly beard.

Then the doctor turned to Caroline and her father. "This is Misha, the radiologist," he said. "He'll take care of the x-ray, once again, and then quickly send me the results so we can move on with our day!" The doctor left the three of them alone.

Caroline remembered meeting the radiologist when she got her first x-ray, and recalled how he gave her a bad feeling, but she was too focused on the pain of her arm then to worry much about him. But now the radiologist gave Caroline the chills, especially when, after getting the explanation from the doctor, he looked over and glared at her like she was a rotten piece of meat, or a fly in his orange juice, or a beard hair in his ice cream.

"Get behind the machine," the radiologist snapped at Caroline, his voice raspy and mean. Caroline looked to her father for help, but her father just shrugged, not sure what to do, and really just wanting to get the x-ray done with and get out of there.

The radiologist, Misha, stroked his wild, greasy beard as he peered down at the instrument panel in front of him. Pushing buttons on the panel, he mumbled and grumbled to himself. His sounds were quite unfriendly, but weren't loud enough for Caroline or her father to understand them.

Suddenly the radiologist yelled, "Now stop moving, girl!" This made Caroline jump, but after that she kept perfectly still until the machine clicked. "Now put your clothes back on and get out," Misha grumbled as he pointed a long bony finger, with a long dirty fingernail at the end of it, toward the door.

After quickly changing out of her gown, Caroline returned with her father to the waiting room. She played a card game with Cora for a few minutes while they waited, until a nurse called her name and led the three of them back to a room where the doctor was waiting.

The doctor's face was pale, all previous color gone, and his eyes were wider than seemed possible. "I, I… I can't explain this," he stammered.

Caroline grinned widely and Cora happily squealed while their father said, "What, doctor? It can't be…"

"It can't be," the doctor agreed. "But it is. It can't be, because we have x-rays from just days ago. And, and I did the surgery myself. I saw the shattered bone, set it. None of this makes any sense. In all my years…" The doctor looked far more terrified than happy, though. In fact, there was no sign of any pleasure on his face whatsoever.

"Are you telling me…" Caroline's father said, bewildered, but far from unhappy.

"Let's just get this cast off," the doctor snapped. "Let's get it off, and then you may leave, and… and… and I just don't know."

The doctor made quick work sawing off the cast. While a few days ago the arm had looked cut and scarred and swollen, now it looked perfectly healthy. While a few days ago the arm had been useless, Caroline unable to move without screaming in pain, now she moved it around and waved it in the air with no hesitation or discomfort at all.

"It's a miracle," her father said, his mouth wide open.

"It's magic, Daddy!" Cora said, smiling and giggling, "I told you, it's unicorn magic!"

Caroline stared at her perfectly healthy arm in amazement, watching in awe as she moved it through the air. She was so happy that tears flowed down her cheeks. Soon her father had the same.

The doctor interrupted the happy moment. "There's no such thing as miracles or magic," he said, voice trembling. "And I have other patients to see. So if you don't mind, it's time for you to leave."

Caroline's father laughed softly at the doctor's lack of composure, and his desire to kick them out. But in his glee the doctor didn't bother him at all, so he just said, "Let's go girls," and they quickly left.

On the drive home, Caroline's father looked back at her through the rear-view mirror. "You're saying... Euni... did this?" he asked.

"Yeah daddy! She came from the woods, and put her horn on me, and used her unicorn magic, and she fixed me, and told me I wasn't broken anymore!" Caroline was giddy with excitement. She looked down at her arm with tender amazement, while Cora pet it like it was itself a furry animal.

"Hm," their father grunted. "Maybe it's time I rethink this whole unicorn thing," he said. "Maybe... maybe it's time I rethink this Euni creature."

Caroline beamed while Cora squealed.

The two girls and their father were too caught up in their wonder and excitement to notice that they were being followed. In a dirty and dented white windowless van behind them, the crazy looking radiologist, Misha, gripped his steering wheel tightly as he followed them home, mumbling nonstop about impossibilities, and magic, and needing to find out more.

Part 3: A New Home

Chapter 14

Caroline, Cora, and their father sat around the small table in their backyard, playing a game of Trouble. Their father popped the die in the middle of the board to roll: 2.

"I just can't get out of the barn!" he complained, throwing his hands into the air. All four of his little blue cylinder pieces were still stuck in Home.

Caroline rolled a 6, smiled, and removed her second piece from Home. She rolled again, a 1, and as she moved the same piece one away from the Start space, she remarked how that roll, the 1 after the 6, always seemed to happen.

After a few quiet moments, Caroline and her father, at the exact same time, said, "Your turn Cora!" Cora was staring off into the forest, as if waiting for someone, or something. Which, in fact, she was.

Cora popped the die with two hands, using the special diamond-shaped hand position she always used when she wanted good luck. She rolled a 6. She didn't have any more pieces at Home to remove, so she moved one of her red pieces into the Finish. "One more then I win!" she yelled. She pushed the dome over the die down again to roll: 2. She moved her last remaining piece onto the blue Start space. "Oh no!" she yelled. "Now I'm a sitting duck! No sixes daddy, no six!"

"As if I could roll a six," he grumbled, pushing down the die bubble. "Six! Haha!" He took his first piece out of Home, and sent Cora's last piece back to her Home.

"Not fair!" Cora yelled, crossing her arms over her chest and pouting.

Caroline laughed at this, which made Cora glare at her, angrily, while her bottom lip turned even more dramatically pouty. Their father rolled again, a 1 ("Of course," he grumbled), and then Caroline rolled a 4. Cora remained sulking at her turn.

"C'mon Cora," her father said. "You're still way in the lead, just roll."

"Hmph," she grunted. "Carolyn wasn't nice. She laughed at me."

"Cora, c'mon, just roll," Caroline snapped. "Stop being such a baby."

"You shouldn't be such a meanie!" Cora said.

Knowing the sisters were getting angrier with one another, and feeling the game was on the verge of falling apart, their father shifted the conversation to one that the girls had been waiting on for days.

"So… this *unicorn* of yours…" their father interrupted, saying the word 'unicorn' full of skepticism, as if he still wasn't convinced. Both girls sat up straight.

"Euni!" Cora said, all her pouting disappearing even faster than it had arrived.

"Ok, *Euni*. If Euni came back, where would you propose to keep her? Because you know, of course, that she can't live in your room anymore."

"She can live in my room!" Cora said.

Their father laughed. "I'm sticking to my rule about no animals in our house," he said. "Not to mention, she's way too big, anyway."

"I agree," Caroline said. "And she was even bigger last time I saw her, when she fixed my arm."

"Even bigger?" Cora asked, eyes wide in amazement.

"So, where would she live?"

"Here, in our backyard?" Caroline asked.

"Would she be happy here?" their father asked, looking around. "It gets cold, and windy, and rains sometimes. I mean, most horses have barns… though to be honest I'm not sure about wild ones… And then there's the question of food. Pets aren't easy, girls. Especially, umm… unicorns?"

"We should just ask Euni!" Cora said.

"How would you ask her?" the girls' father asked.

"Carolyn can talk to her! Euni speaks!"

"*Really*, Caroline?" their father said, voice now full of amusement in addition to doubt. "You could just ask her?"

"I could try," said Caroline, ignoring his tone.

Their father looked around, smirking. "I gotta see this," he said. "Well, is she nearby? Would she come to you if you call her? Or how does that work?"

"I have no idea," Caroline said. "She showed up out of nowhere to fix my arm. Which maybe means she was close, but was probably afraid to be, well, caught. So, I guess I could try."

"Try!" Cora yelled. "Try calling for her! Euni! Euneeeeee!"

Caroline looked to her father, who shrugged his shoulders and extended the palm of his hand as if to say, "Go ahead."

Caroline stood up, and yelled, "Euni! Euneee! *Caroline Euni Ama*!" She felt a little silly using Euni's language when Euni understood English so well, but also thought it might get her attention.

A minute later there was a rustling of leaves in the forest. Cora and her father joined Caroline in standing.

"*Euni Carolyn Ama!*" the unicorn cheerfully brayed as she galloped out from among the trees.

Chapter 15

"*Euni Ema Zapaku Dattu,*" Euni said to Cora and Caroline's father, who was in shock, and having trouble believing his eyes (and ears).

"She says she needs a soft bed," Caroline said.

"You can really understand that?" her father said, amazed. "All I hear is *Euni Paka Data Paka Data Maka!*"

Cora bent over giggling, while Euni tilted her head in confusion.

Caroline laughed, then answered, "I understand most of what she says by now. But I am still learning, and do need to ask Euni to teach me words pretty often."

Even Cora was in awe of how much of Euni's strange language Caroline had picked up.

As Euni spoke, explaining what she wanted for her new home in the backyard, Caroline did her best to translate for her father. Occasionally Euni had to stop and explain a word or phrase to Caroline, but Caroline was fairly quick in figuring out the translations to Euni's words.

"Okay, I think I got it all," their father said, looking at his notes. "A soft bed, a little hut to protect the bed from the weather, and a fence to keep other big animals out."

"*Eee!*" Euni brayed, sounding pleased.

"That means yes," Caroline explained.

"Yeah I figured that one out," her father said with a wink. "And then for food, you said now that she's grown, she can find things to eat and drink in the forest by herself?"

"That's what she said," Caroline said, and Euni agreed.

"Then let's go to the store!" their father said. Caroline and Cora squealed in delight and hugged him tightly while saying "thank you thank you thank you" over and over again. Even Euni stuck her big head into the group hug to show her appreciation.

"We can also pick up some stuff for your birthday party next month, Caroline," he said, which made Caroline jump up and down and give him another big hug.

"I want the theme to be unicorns!" she said.

"Yeah, unicorns!" Cora echoed.

Their father laughed. "Of course," he said. He didn't have the heart in that moment to tell his girls that he didn't think it was a good idea to have Euni around during the birthday party – or, really, any time other people were around. He could just imagine how people would react to Euni, good and bad, but decided to wait to have that conversation with his daughters.

It took them a few days to build Euni's new home, which consisted of a round wooden roof held up by two walls, a short wooden fence around the open area, and a thick foam mat on the ground under the roof. The foam mat was large enough to fit Euni comfortably, and Caroline covered it with the fur blanket that she once bought for Euni to sleep on in her room.

The girls' father, of course, did most of the building, but the girls helped as much as they could. They dug holes for the posts, held up pieces of wood while their father drilled them, and hammered nails here and there to make sure things were strong.

Euni once offered to assist, saying to Caroline's father, "*Euni Fanata?*"

Caroline spent a minute with Euni to figure out that *Fanata* meant help, and then translated for her father before adding the new word to her notebook. But after looking down at Euni's hooves, her father replied, "I think we have it covered Euni, but thank you." So Euni mostly looked on, pleased, occasionally teaching Caroline new words, or being pet by Cora, whenever the girls took a break from helping their father.

None of them had any idea that, deep in the forest, the crazy radiologist Misha was hiding out, spending hours every day watching them through his binoculars.

Chapter 16

Euni was officially back in Caroline and Cora's life, and their excitement and fun with her was endless - at least when they were at home, and allowed to play with Euni. Their days spent at school were hard, with both girls having trouble concentrating on their lessons, thinking over and over again how wonderful it was to have a pet unicorn, and imagining all the things they wanted to do with Euni once they got home.

At home they would ride Euni around the backyard, and pet her, and clean her hair, and play silly games like hopscotch and baby-care (the three of them each taking turns being the baby) and doctor and air-conditioning and tag.

One day, while playing hide-and-go-seek, Cora ran into the forest and hid in a spot that happened to be very close to Misha's hiding spot. When Cora approached, Misha quickly covered his entire body with his camouflage blanket, and while Cora hid herself by pressing up against a nearby tree, Misha held his breath, terrified he was going to get caught. If he got caught, Misha knew his plan would be ruined. Luckily (for him!) Cora was terrible at hide-and-go-seek: Caroline heard Cora giggling from afar and found her without having to get close, and, therefore, without discovering Misha.

So Misha was able to keep watching, and keep taking notes: *Thursday 4:00-5:00, more ridiculous games. Today: hide and seek. The horned beast remained in the yard.*

The hardest times every day for Cora and Caroline were when they had to say goodbye to Euni, which was both in the morning when they left to go to school, and at night when it was time to go inside. Their father made them eat dinner as a family in the house – it was their time to talk about their days, to connect with one another, to celebrate the good things in their lives, and to work together through the bad.

And Misha would take note: *5:45 dinner, same time as always. The girls and father indoors, and the beast in the yard as usual.*

After dinner (plus sometimes a game if they ate quickly and thoroughly!), and before bath and bedtime, the girls would call their mother in Australia to say goodnight/goodmorning. While their father did tell Cora and Caroline they shouldn't tell their friends at school about Euni ("It will make them too jealous, and jealous kids usually don't make nice friends"), he didn't tell them (yet!) that Euni should be a complete secret - so they told their mother everything about their pet unicorn.

Their mother, however, didn't believe any of it. To her daughters' stories she would simply respond, "You girls have quite the imagination! Sounds like you're having fun!" To which the two sisters would giggle and shrug their shoulders.

Whenever they weren't with Euni, the girls assumed that she stayed in their backyard, remaining in or around her new home. But this wasn't actually the case. Often at night, after the girls were asleep, Euni would grow lonely and sad, wondering where all the other unicorns in the world could be.

Euni didn't yet know that, at that time, there were no other unicorns like her in the world - at least not in this world, the Real World, since almost all unicorns live in the Land of Unicorns. Euni didn't know that she, as a tiny rainbow frog, had come from that Land of Unicorns. Euni also had no idea, of course, that she had been sent to the Real World from the Land of Unicorns to find a child to save them. And she wouldn't learn of the Land of Unicorns, or her responsibility, until well after her first birthday.

But not knowing any of that, and longing for the company of other unicorns, and for a family of her own, Euni would often grow sad at night. Feeling alone and lonely, she wondered where her parents were, who her parents were, and where all the other unicorns, or even rainbow frogs, could be.

And often on those nights, when she was unable to sleep, Euni would wander into the forest, to the creek where Caroline had found her as a baby rainbow frog. And there Euni would look around, and make soft sad unicorn noises, and hope that she would get some sort of unicorn response.

But she never did.

And because Euni took these walks secretly, late at night, neither Caroline nor Cora nor their father had any idea. In fact, there was only one person in the whole world that knew about Euni's sad trips to the creek in the forest.

Smiling widely through his wiry, disheveled beard, Misha wrote in his notebook: *Wednesday, 2am, horned beast returns to the exact same spot by the creek. Family asleep.*

"It's time," he mumbled to himself.

Chapter 17

With Caroline's birthday just a week away, the girls spent a lot of their time with Euni planning. Caroline wrote list after list, thinking and planning and helping her father by considering exactly how she wanted things to be. She wrote guest lists and drew invitations. She sketched a map of the backyard, where her birthday would take place, and drew exactly where she wanted each activity. On the map, inside her sketch of Euni's backyard home, Caroline drew a picture of herself blowing out birthday candles on an enormous cake. *Can your friend Gerald bake my cake?* she wrote on a note for her father. *He makes the best cakes! And ask him for rainbows and unicorns on it please!*

Caroline also wrote down ideas of where Euni could go during the party, in order to make sure that her relatives, friends, and friends' families wouldn't find out about the unicorn. Then she made lists of possible stories that she could tell her guests about Euni's home, and what it was. But, unable to come up with anything too clever, and not wanting to lie too much, Caroline decided she would just tell people the truth: that it was a unicorn home. She was sure that her guests, like her mother, would think it was part of her pretend games, like a fake kitchen or a big dollhouse. And she would let them.

While Caroline spent her days doing her planning, Misha spent his nights doing his. Under the cover of darkness, the crazy radiologist used a flashlight to review his intricate sketches of the creek area in the forest behind Caroline's house. Plodding through the mud in rubber boots, and still wearing his white lab coat, Misha carefully laid down nets in the mud near the creek, and tied knots in long strands of rope that he secured to trees and was careful to hide.

"It's ready," he mumbled to himself one night, stroking his long messy beard. "And just in time."

And sure enough, within a couple of hours, Euni took one of her sad, longing walks into the forest, wondering where all the other unicorns could be. She meandered along the side of the creek, head down, looking into the mud in the hopes of seeing a rainbow frog, while making sad groaning unicorn calls.

No one answered Euni's calls, for there were no other unicorns, or rainbow frogs, to answer. Nor were there any people around to hear her sad sounds - the closest people, other than Misha, were Caroline and her family, who were in their beds, sound asleep.

Which is also why, as a rope cinched around her front hoof, and a net lifted her two hind legs into the air, no one other than Misha heard Euni's terrified unicorn shrieks.

Chapter 18

Caroline was immediately worried when Euni wasn't in the backyard in the morning. "Something's wrong," she told Cora and then their father. Cora got worried too, her lips twisting in concern, but didn't know what to say or do.

Their father was dismissive. "I'm sure she's fine, sweetie," he said.

"She's not fine," Caroline argued. "She's there every morning, there in the home we built for her."

"She's an animal, Caroline," her father said, sipping his coffee, getting a little annoyed. "Maybe she felt like sleeping somewhere else. Or maybe she went for an early walk. Now go eat your eggs, it's almost time for school."

Caroline sat and poked at her eggs with her fork, far too anxious to have an appetite. Thinking that her father was wrong, knowing that she understood Euni best, Caroline wondered what could have happened to her pet unicorn.

"Maybe she went to get you a birthday present for your party tomorrow," her father said with a small, hopeful laugh.

But Caroline didn't laugh, or even smile.

Seeing the worry in Caroline's face, her father came to her, knelt down, and put his arm around her shoulders. "Listen," he said. "If Euni isn't back by the time you get home from school, we'll figure out what to do, together. I'll help." He said it even as he wondered what there was to do.

"Okay," Caroline mumbled, knowing that was really her only option.

Sneaking underneath their father's arm, Cora came and gave Caroline a big hug. "I love you Carolyn," she said through a messy mouthful of eggs.

"I love you too," Caroline said, forcing a smile, and hugging both Cora and their father.

Meanwhile, during this scene of familial love and support, Euni was frantically running and jumping around a small fenced-in area, screaming *"Fanata! Carolyn, Fanataaa!"* If Caroline were nearby, she would have heard this as Euni screaming for her to help.

Misha, smiling broadly, stroked his long scraggly beard as he looked on at Euni from the other side of the fence. Misha was a very tall man, so tall that kids would point at him (before growing scared of him), but the fence was even taller. It was constructed using metal posts so that Euni wouldn't be able to break them and escape, and the metal posts were close enough together so that Euni wouldn't be able to squeeze out between them.

"I did it," Misha said to himself, almost laughing. "I actually, finally did it. A real live unicorn! And all mine!"

"*Fanataaa!*" Euni screamed. She wondered if Caroline would notice the long lines on the forest floor, the lines Euni made by dragging her hooves while Misha yanked her through the forest to this cage.

"Oh shush now you beast," Misha hollered. "We're just getting started." And then mumbling more to himself again, he said, "I can't wait to see what kind of magic you're capable of. I'll show them your magic abilities, and they'll never laugh at me again! No, this time I'll be the scientist laughing! Hahahahaha!"

"*Niii! Fanataa! Caroliiinnn!*"

"No one can hear you way out here," Misha said to Euni. "So you might as well get comfortable. Because this, you magic creature… you beast that's going to make me famous… this here," he lifted his arms toward the metal fenced-in pen, "*This* is your new home!"

Part 4: Caroline to the Rescue

Chapter 19

Caroline couldn't focus at school that day, and was eventually sent to the principal's office for ignoring her teacher. But Caroline didn't care. She knew, deep inside, that her best friend was in trouble, so she couldn't help but worry, and try to come up with ways to save Euni.

The principal called Caroline's father due to his concern for Caroline's "uncharacteristic despondence." These were words that, to Caroline, sounded just as foreign as new words from Euni. She didn't know that the principal's words meant that Caroline wasn't her normal joyful self, and rather seemed sad and hopeless.

Caroline thought about figuring out the principal's weird words in the same way she figured out Euni's new words, and she initially smiled. But then she grew even more sad, more despondent, when she remembered that Euni was missing, and likely in trouble.

Fortunately, Caroline's father responded sympathetically to the principal's call, thanking him and saying that he would discuss it with Caroline when she got home. For her father, of course, knew the problem, and, since he worked from home, he also knew that Euni still hadn't returned. He even spent some time that day thinking of solutions himself.

Caroline had some hope that Euni would be back when she got home, so began crying when she saw the empty backyard.

Her father was expecting Caroline's reaction, and quickly gave her a firm hug. Cora, with a pouty lip, ran to join the two of them, squeezing her sister tightly.

Then their father went into solution mode. "I know you're sad and worried," he said to his daughters, "but worrying and crying isn't going to help Euni."

Caroline sniffled, not knowing what to say, but also knowing he was right.

"So, let's think, and plan," he said to Caroline and Cora. "Starting with, what are the most likely things to have happened to Euni?"

Caroline shrugged, her tears still falling, though silently now. Cora copied her sister with a big shrug of her own.

"Well, first, it could be what I said this morning," their father said. "That she's just off somewhere else, maybe looking for food, or maybe with a new friend, or something like that."

"No!" Caroline snapped. "Something is wrong!"

"Caroline," her father said sternly. "Right now we're making a list of possibilities, okay? Next step will be judging the possibilities, and thinking about what we can do about them, but for now let's list everything that *could* be true, okay?"

"Okay," Caroline grumbled.

Their father wrote on a pad of paper: *1. Off on her own.* "Give me more possibilities," he said.

"Someone stole her," Caroline said bitterly. "Or she's in the forest, hurt."

"Good," their father said, adding to his list: *2. Stolen 3. Wounded.*

"Maybe she went back to wherever unicorns come from," Cora said. Then she shrugged. "Maybe it was just time. I mean, how did she even get here in the first place."

Caroline grimaced at this, scared that it could be true.

But their father said, "Great," and wrote: *4. Went Home to the Land of Unicorns.* "Any other possibilities?" he asked them.

"She could be lost?" Cora said.

"Good." *5. Lost*

"Maybe she's helping someone," Caroline said, now done crying, and busy thinking. "Like, someone else got hurt like I did, and Euni needed to help them."

"Perfect," *6. On a mission.* Her father smirked at this one. "Anything else?"

The three of them sat in silence for a minute before their father said, "Okay, sounds like these are the possibilities. Now, let's think about what we'd do in the case of each possibility."

Caroline smiled, seeing her father's way of calmly coming up with strategies. "It's like a game of chess," she thought to herself.

"So if Euni's off on her own, possibility number one, what would we do," he asked them.

"Wait for her?" Cora asked.

"Or look for her," Caroline said quickly.

"Ok great," he said, writing down *Wait at home* and *Search for Euni* beneath the underlined word *Solutions.* "And possibility 2, what would we do if she was stolen?"

"Search?" Caroline said.

"Good," her father said. "But maybe a little differently, right? Cuz I imagine she wouldn't be easy to steal, and wouldn't go without a fight… so we'd search, but maybe we'd look a little closer?"

"Yeah," Caroline said, growing a little excited. "Like, look for clues!"

"Exactly," her father said, writing *Search for clues* in the solutions list. "And if she's wounded?"

"Look for her!" Cora said.

"Yes," said their father. "And we already have that on our solutions list, so we're good if that's the case. And if she's lost, we'd do the same, right?"

"Yeah!" the girls said together.

"And if she's on a mission, or back in the Land of Unicorns, what would we do?"

"We'd have to wait, I guess," Caroline said. "And hope."

"Exactly," their father said, "and we already have that solution option, waiting at home, written down." He handed the list to Caroline. "So for all the worrying we could do, and all the reasons we could think of as to why she's gone, it looks like the only action to take is to search the forest, for Euni or for clues, and if that doesn't work, then we have no choice but to wait."

Caroline nodded, so Cora nodded too, and their father continued, "And really, if we're looking for clues, we're bound to find Euni if she's around. So in the end, there's actually only one thing we can do. Search the forest for signs of Euni. And if we can't find anything, we're forced to just wait for her."

"True," Caroline mumbled, wondering if their father had come to that conclusion before they even started talking.

Chapter 20

"We only have one hour before it gets dark," Caroline and Cora's father said, "and at that point we'll have to call off the search for now, and go eat dinner and do our bedtime stuff."

"That's not long enough!" Caroline argued. "We can bring flashlights! And we don't have school tomorrow, so we can stay up later!"

"It's not safe," their father said. "And you girls need to eat, and call your mother, and get some rest. Don't forget that your birthday party is tomorrow, Caroline, and I don't want you all tired and grouchy for that."

Caroline stomped her foot and started to pout in protest. "How could I have a birthday party with Euni missing," she thought.

"But how about this," her father said. "If Euni's still missing, first thing tomorrow you can start looking again, and can search all morning before your birthday party."

"But Euni's in trouble now!" Caroline whined. She felt herself becoming angry; felt her emotions growing bigger.

Her father noticed as well. "Caroline, I'm not going to argue with you. If you want my help, you need to pull it together. We have one hour to look right now, and we're wasting it. If we have to wait until the morning to find her, we're only talking about one night, and you know Euni can take care of herself. I mean, she can probably take care of herself better than you can take care of her. She is a unicorn, after all."

Part of Caroline wanted to keep arguing, the angry frustrated part of her, but another part of her knew that she was wasting time, time that could be spent in search of Euni.

So Caroline took three big breaths, each time breathing out as slowly as she could. The technique was something she had learned to be a great way to regain control of herself when her emotions were taking over.

When she finally felt composed, Caroline put on her jacket and boots and headed out the door. Cora silently did the same, following her sister outside. Their father left the house last, letting his daughters lead the search.

And for one hour they scoured the forest near their home, calling for Euni while quickly looking as widely as they could in the small amount of time they had.

They found nothing. No Euni, no Euni sounds, and no clues as to what could have happened.

"Time to go eat," their father eventually said. Neither girl responded. "I made lasagna, your favorite, for a little pre-birthday dinner treat."

"We haven't even made it to the creek," Caroline said. "Maybe she went…"

"If she was at the creek she'd hear us," their father interrupted. "And we'd hear her. Time to go home now, girls."

"But…"

"No buts. Let's go. Now."

So the three of them turned around and walked home, their father leading the way. Caroline and Cora dragged their feet in the dirt and kicked up dust with every step, leaving long scratches in the forest floor behind them.

About a mile away, deep in the forest, Euni lay in Misha's pen on the cold, hard dirt, and quietly cried. For a little while she thought she could hear Caroline's voice yelling for her, and she tried screaming back. But no one came, and before long the sounds disappeared.

Chapter 21

Caroline tossed and turned in her bed, unable to sleep. She imagined Euni in all sorts of trouble, crying out for Caroline's help while Caroline lay warm, comfortable, and safe in her bed.

As much as Caroline wanted to get out of bed and keep looking, she could imagine her father's response if she wasn't home when he woke up. She knew he'd be terrified - more worried about Caroline than even Caroline was worried about Euni.

But after hours spent trying, and failing, to fall asleep, Caroline couldn't take it anymore. She needed to keep looking for Euni, even if it meant getting into the most trouble she had ever been in. She had to do everything she could, and decided, considering how much time she generally spent in the forest by herself, that if she left her father a note he'd be less worried.

"He did say first thing in the morning," she thought, trying to justify what she was about to do. And in the middle of the night, in the earliest hours of her tenth birthday, Caroline put on her jacket, grabbed a flashlight, and wrote down the following:

Dear Daddy. I went to look for Euni. Please don't be worried or mad. I promise I'll be safe, and back in time for my party. I love you so much! Caroline

Caroline cringed as she pictured how worried her father was going to be, but then she had another idea. She wrote a second note, this one to her sister. Caroline left the note on her own bed, and put the note to her father underneath it. Then she ventured outside, into the cold and dark night.

Caroline grew immediately afraid, realizing she had never been outside so early, well before the sunrise. Everything around her, from the ground to the trees to her own home, seemed spooky, haunted, and ghostly under the thin moonlight.

"I need to check the creek," she whispered to herself, building up her courage, and she walked into the forest, flashlight shining straight ahead.

Every noise scared her. Every time she heard anything, she would spin the flashlight toward it, look hard, and whisper, "Euni?" But each time there was nothing there, nothing to respond. And every time a branch touched her arm or leg she jumped, and slapped it away, thinking it was a hand.

But Caroline was brave and determined, and soon made it to the creek.

Her boots made a squishy crackling noise on the muddy ground around the creek, which was slightly frozen over in the cold of the night. "Euneeee," Caroline called, louder now, knowing she was far enough from her home for her family to not be able to hear her.

She walked along the creek, shining her flashlight into the bushes nearby, against the trees, and on the mud. She began shivering out of a mixture of cold and exhaustion, and soon began wishing she was back in her bed.

"What are you doing," Caroline asked herself.

But then she saw it. Dangling from a tree in front of her, gently swaying just above her head, was a rope. The end of it was frayed, like it had been cut in a hurry.

She pointed her flashlight to the ground underneath the rope, and saw a violent looking mess etched into the partially frozen mud. There were lines, each a few feet long, cut deep into the mud. Getting closer with her flashlight, Caroline saw the shape of a hoof at the end of each muddy line.

"Euni," she whispered, terrified. Then she saw the heavy boot prints in the mud a couple feet away, and the splashes of mud scattered all around. "Who…"

Looking to where the mud seemed to splash the widest, Caroline noticed a trail of more deep hoof scratches trailing into the forest on the far side of the creek. So she jumped over a narrow part of the creek and began walking, deeper into the forest, deeper than she had ever gone before, following the trail of lines that Caroline was sure Euni had left for her to find.

"I'm coming," Caroline whispered, as she walked further and further away from her home.

Chapter 22

Finally, just as the whispers of morning sun began to appear on the horizon, Caroline reached a clearing in the trees, the clearing that Euni's hoof scratches had led her to.

After her long walk through the forest Caroline was no longer cold, though her eyes stung with lack of sleep and her legs wobbled in exhaustion. But when Caroline looked into the clearing in the forest and saw the rundown farmhouse, her mind immediately woke up in excitement, anxiety, and fear.

"Where am I," she wondered, biting her lip.

Next to the farmhouse, and at the end of the trail of hoof scratches in the dirt, Caroline saw the tall metal fence. She immediately ran toward it, and even before she got to the fence she saw Euni lying on the ground beyond it.

Caroline turned her flashlight off. She glanced briefly at the nearby farmhouse, barely lit by the twilight, before whispering as loud as she could through the fence to her sleeping unicorn: "Euni!"

While the metal bars were close enough to one another to keep Euni inside, Caroline had no problem climbing through the fence and into the large pen.

"Euni! It's me!" she whispered forcefully.

Euni opened her eyes softly and looked up. When she saw Caroline, Euni jumped to her feet and galloped over. "*Carolyn!!*" Euni brayed. "*Carolyn Ghee Euni Fanata!*"

"Shh!" Caroline said, while hugging Euni. "Of course I came to help you." She looked around the fenced-in area. "But now we need to figure out a way to get out of here!"

Caroline watched Euni as the unicorn looked past her, looked to see if Caroline brought help, brought her father, or brought any other way to get Euni out of the cage. And when Caroline saw Euni's eyes become a mixture of sad and scared upon seeing no other help, upon discovering that Caroline came alone, she realized what a mistake she had made by coming all the way out here all by herself. No one knew where she was, and really, she had no way of actually helping Euni.

For a moment Caroline panicked, her chest tightening in fear, but then she had an idea. "Now I know where you are," she said to Euni, trying her best to sound confident and reassuring. "All I need to do is follow your tracks back home, and then I can get help."

Euni dropped her head at the thought of being left alone again with the crazy radiologist. Her eyes gazed sadly at the ground between her and Caroline.

"I'll be quick!" Caroline assured her, patting Euni's shoulder. She took a step back, ready to leave and go get help, when suddenly she heard a loud *clunk*, and a bright light filled the area.

It was suddenly so bright that it seemed the sun had darted up into the sky. But looking around, Caroline saw that only Euni's pen had filled with light. And looking up, Caroline saw that the brightness came from a huge set of lights on the barn that reminded her of the lights at a baseball stadium. The lights were so bright that it hurt Caroline's eyes to look up at them, so she quickly looked down again, scared and confused and now having difficulty seeing.

Caroline was rubbing her eyes when she heard an angry grizzled roar come from the direction of the old barn: "You!"

With her eyes still dazzled by the bright lights, when Caroline looked in the direction of the voice, she could only see the outline of a person walking toward the pen.

"What do you think you're doing?" the furious voice yelled. "How did you get here?"

Between the tall silhouette of the person and the dreadful sound of his voice, Caroline quickly realized who it was, realized who had stolen Euni and put her in this cage.

"The radiologist…" Caroline said, terrified. She was just starting to be able to see the white lab coat beneath the scraggly beard. "Misha…"

"That's right!" Misha yelled, now standing just outside the metal posts of the pen. "But I'm a scientist! Being a radiologist just paid the bills, while I searched… while I found something that would change the world!" Misha, the mad scientist, laughed maniacally.

Caroline stepped back toward Euni, pressing her body against her unicorn even as she knew that she should run. But Caroline also knew that she couldn't run, couldn't leave Euni alone with this crazy scientist.

"And now, now I have that greatness coming," Misha bellowed, lifting his arms into the air. "Now I'm going to change the world!"

Caroline saw that Misha was holding a long net with one of his lifted hands.

"And you, little girl, you should not have come here!" At this, Misha bent down and climbed into the pen that held Caroline and Euni.

Chapter 23

Back at home, while Misha was climbing through the fence that surrounded Euni and Caroline with a net in his hand, Cora was just waking up. She always woke up with the sunrise, no matter what time it was. Since it was winter the sun rose later in the morning, so upon waking up Cora was immediately surprised that Caroline wasn't already up and making noise. It was Caroline's birthday, after all, and her birthday party was just hours away.

"Also," Cora thought to herself, "I figured Carolyn would wake me and Daddy up early to go searching for Euni, so we'd have as much time as possible before her party."

So Cora walked to Caroline's room, full of confused curiosity. She was shocked when she saw her sister's room, and her bed, empty. "Daddeeeee!" Cora yelled.

"Yes sweetie?" her father yelled back from downstairs.

"Carolyn's not here!" Cora replied. Then she saw the note on Caroline's bed.

"I can't hear you," her father yelled, in the annoyed voice that Cora knew meant he wasn't really awake yet. "Gimme a minute, I'm making coffee."

Cora read the note, which began: *Dear Cora: I went to search for Euni, and I need your help so Daddy doesn't get worried…*

As Cora finished reading the note, her father walked into Caroline's room behind her. He was rubbing the sleep from his eyes with one hand, carrying a mug of steaming coffee with the other. Cora quickly hid her note in her pajama pants before he noticed it.

"Where's Caroline?" he asked, yawning dramatically.

"She, uh, just left… just now… to go look for Euni."

"So early?" he asked. "Without saying goodbye?"

"She said she thought you wouldn't mind cuz you said she could go looking first thing in the morning. And, she left you this note." Cora handed her father Caroline's note to him.

"Hm," he said, and took a loud sip of his coffee, the kind of sip the girls loved to imitate and make fun of. "I guess I did say first thing." He read her note, and then shrugged. "I guess she wouldn't miss her own birthday party. Kay I'm gonna go take a shower."

As he left Cora grew nervous, mostly because she hadn't told her father the whole truth. But she told herself that it was a small lie, barely a lie, because she truly had no idea what time Caroline left the house - and it was still possible that Caroline did leave just before Cora woke up. But Cora was also nervous knowing that Caroline may have left earlier, may have even left the house while it was still dark out, and that was just plain scary for her to think about.

Her father was also a bit nervous. Why hadn't Caroline said goodbye? And was she going to be safe searching by herself? But he reminded himself that Caroline spent a lot of her time alone in the forest behind their home, playing and exploring and searching for strange animals. Therefore, most of all he was nervous that a missing unicorn was going to ruin his daughter's birthday.

So even though they were both a little worried, Cora and her father knew (or thought they knew!) that Caroline was somewhere in her favorite forest, somewhere where she knew her way around far better than either of them did.

But Caroline, of course, was no longer anywhere familiar in the forest. Caroline was over a mile away, huddling against Euni, beginning to cry for her father and sister, and wishing she had never left home.

Cora bit her lip nervously, hoping that Caroline would make it home before her birthday party began.

Chapter 24

"You should never have come here!" Misha growled at Caroline, as he slowly walked toward her like a stalking predator. He stared directly at her, his eyes looking crazy, while he carefully unfolded the net in his hands.

Caroline trembled in fear, more scared than she had ever been before. "He's right," she thought to herself as she began to cry. "I should have never come here. Should have never come alone. Should have never asked Cora to lie for me. Should have never disobeyed Daddy." Caroline was so terrified, so overwhelmed, that she was having trouble breathing, and gasped for every breath.

"*Ghee Roopee!*" Euni said suddenly.

"Go where?" Caroline asked, turning her head to her friend.

Euni lowered her body by kneeling onto her front knees. "*Ghee Roopee Euni!*" she brayed. "*Ema Carolyn Ghee Roopee Euni! Roopeeee!*"

Carolyn finally understood: *Roopee* must mean "on" or "up"! With Misha the mad scientist just steps away now, getting ready to throw the net over her, Caroline scrambled onto Euni's lowered back.

Misha quickly threw his net, but Euni immediately stood up again, and the net hit harmlessly against the unicorn's side.

Misha made a loud, frustrated snarling noise and ran forward. He reached out for Caroline's foot, but Euni started galloping, so Misha grabbed air instead of her foot.

Then Misha began chasing them, but the fenced-in area was just large enough for Euni to run around the perimeter of it while avoiding Misha's grasp.

Finally, panting for air, Misha gave up chasing them. He climbed back out of the pen through the metal fence, and jogged back to the barn.

"Maybe I should run now, run home," Caroline said to both Euni and to herself. She still didn't want to leave Euni behind, but she was now deeply terrified for her own safety in addition to Euni's. Caroline was also worried, though, that if she ran Misha would chase after her, and that without Euni's quickness he'd be able to catch her.

Caroline's indecision didn't matter, because moments later Misha reappeared. This time he was carrying a much larger net, a net big enough to catch Euni in addition to Caroline. It was, in fact, the same net Misha had used to capture Euni in the first place.

Euni bucked and brayed, now also full of terror - both for herself and for her best friend, Caroline.

"There's no way you can jump?" Caroline asked Euni, trying her best to think of something, anything, to get them out, to get them away from the mad scientist. "Or, break the posts?"

"*Niii!*" Euni brayed.

Chapter 25

Caroline gave up, knowing that within a minute Misha would have his net over both her and Euni, and she collapsed forward against her unicorn's broad shoulders. She wrapped her arms around Euni's neck, hugged her firmly, and again began to cry. Caroline was so scared, so disappointed in herself, and so sorry for not being honest with her sister and father. And her tears flowed, down her cheeks, and down onto Euni's rainbow-colored mane and shimmering white hair.

Euni felt Caroline's tears, and then thought then about how badly she had wanted a family, how she had spent all those nights crying for more unicorns, when in reality she already had a family. Caroline was like a mother to her, caring for Euni and tending to all her needs from the very beginning. When Euni was in trouble, Caroline had found her clues and traced her path all the way through the forest. Euni recognized how Caroline had risked herself in order to try to save her. And thinking of Cora, and the girls' father, Euni realized that she already had the love a family, a family that cared for her, and had given her a home.

Euni suddenly knew: she didn't have to search for a family, or for love. It had been there the whole time. She had had it the whole time. She just hadn't realized it.

At that moment Euni was overwhelmed by a tremendous sense of love, followed by a tremendous sense of responsibility - the responsibility unique to members of a family. And with Misha now climbing back into the pen through the fence, Euni realized something else about herself, something else that she already had inside of her, something that had always been part of her potential, of who she was and what she had, even if she had never realized it before.

As Caroline held her and sobbed, and as Misha angrily approached, Euni closed her eyes and focused on that hidden piece of herself, that something else that she had never before been aware of. Taking a deep breath in, Euni felt the areas of her body between her spine and stomach, right behind Caroline's knees, start to tingle, and then separate, and then extend.

The feeling was strange, like growing new arms suddenly. It was a sensation unlike any that Euni had experienced before, but she instinctively knew it was right.

Euni also knew that she needed to hurry, so she tried to push her body, to put pressure on the once invisible new areas of herself, to help her transformation along.

And within seconds, Euni had grown magnificent white wings. The fronts of the huge wings were covered by a smooth shimmery silver surface, while the backs were laced with long white feathers, each nearly the length of Euni's legs.

Caroline felt the eruption behind her knees. At first she cringed and squeezed tighter onto Euni's neck, thinking that Misha was already there and grabbing at her. But Caroline quickly realized that whatever was happening felt far larger and more magical than anything the crazy scientist could do. So she sat up, face puffy and red from her crying, and looked beside her, where she saw Euni's magical glistening unicorn wings.

Misha cried "Whaaa?" His mouth and eyes gaped open like an angry goldfish. But soon he grew serious again, looking amazed but more intent than ever. He prepared to cast his net, and lunged forward toward Euni and Caroline.

Just as Misha threw his net at them, Euni gave her wings a giant flap. The gust of air from her massive wings knocked Misha to the ground, while his net flew backward through the air and landed on top of him.

The second flap of Euni's wings lifted her a few feet into the air. Caroline panicked for a moment, and then quickly reached around Euni's neck again so she wouldn't fall.

Euni flapped her wings again, and then again, pushing her and Caroline higher each time. The flapping began to speed up as Euni got a better feel for her wings, and her wings grew stronger with every beat.

Soon the two were fully airborne, flying away from the mad scientist, who was left cursing and waving his fist from underneath his own net. Caroline watched him grow smaller and smaller as they flew further away, with greater and greater speed.

Caroline and Euni made great happy whooping noises, overcome by the joy of their escape, and by the magic of unicorns.

Part 5: The Long Way Home

Chapter 26

Euni drifted like an eagle over the open ocean, taking great pleasure in her speed through the sky, the wind in her face, the feel of Caroline's arms around her shoulders, and the freedom gained in flying away from the mad scientist, Misha.

Caroline rested her face on Euni's rainbow crest, smelling the tangy citrus smell of Euni's skin and hair. She was still stunned at what had happened, still jittery from the greatest scare she had ever experienced, but at the same time Caroline was full of absolute relief and in awe of the magic and power of Euni.

Caroline had learned about animal instincts before, the things they are born already knowing how to do, in addition to the abilities that animals inherit across generations. She loved monarch butterflies, and remembered how amazed she was when she learned about their migrations: monarchs fly thousands of miles south, and three generations later, long after the death of the original butterflies, they fly back north – back to the exact same tree that their great grandparents came from.

Caroline thought about how Euni's language was probably similar. As far as Caroline knew, Euni had never met another unicorn, so her ability to speak must have been instinctual, or something she knew naturally without ever being taught. Like a bird's song, in a way, but more amazing.

"At the same time," Caroline thought, "Euni's ability to fly, and her realizing it just in time, just when we needed it most, was absolutely magical."

And since it was unicorn magic, Caroline assumed then that all unicorns could fly. But she didn't know (yet!) that every unicorn had different magic powers - that not all of them could magically heal things, like Euni had done to her broken arm. Caroline wouldn't learn that aspect of unicorns until Euni had her babies - and even then, she wouldn't really understand the marvelous abilities and magic that unicorns could have, and that would remain in their horns, until she finally visited the Land of Unicorns.

Suddenly Caroline remembered that it was her birthday, and recalled her notes to Cora, and to their father. Her heart sank in her chest. At the very least, Caroline knew she needed to get home in time for her birthday party, or else she'd be in big trouble.

Yelling over the roaring wind, Caroline hollered, "Euni, I think it's time to go home now!"

"*Eee*," Euni brayed, flapping her giant wings and turning around in the sky. Just like an animal remembering something it already knew, Euni had quickly grown comfortable using her wings.

But after turning around in the sky, all either of them could see was ocean all around. Euni flew so incredibly fast that there was no longer any land in sight.

"Akur Hitimi?" Euni asked.

"Where's home?" Caroline yelled, her eyes growing wide. "I thought you knew where home was! I'm not the one flying."

"Mina," Euni said shyly, apologizing. *"Mina Carolyn, Minaaa."* She was no monarch butterfly.

"It's okay," Caroline said, looking to their left toward the rising sun, wondering what time it was. "Let's just hurry back to land, and hopefully we'll see home." She had no idea if they were even heading the right direction, though. "Or we can land, and ask for directions," she said, nervously.

Euni beat her wings forcefully, flying faster and faster over the water, searching for land.

Chapter 27

Eventually, of course, Caroline and Euni did see land. But as they approached it Caroline immediately knew that it wasn't the right land, wasn't familiar land, and most importantly, that it wasn't land they could use to figure out their way home. Also disturbing to Caroline was that the air was suddenly warm, warm enough that she decided to take off her jacket.

The land was covered in a dense blanket of trees, with rivers here and there cutting curved lines like long snakes through the jungle. Although Caroline didn't know much about trees, didn't even know the names of the types of trees near her home other than the redwoods, she knew that she had never seen trees like these, or a forest like this. And as far as she could see in the distance, these giant tropical looking trees covered the earth.

"Minaua," Euni said again, realizing the same thing as Caroline: that they were very far from home.

"Look!" Caroline said after a few seconds of flying in silence. "Some houses! Let's land and ask how to get back to California."

Euni, using her wings to slow down as they approached, drifted toward the cluster of homes that were nearly hidden in the thick forest. As they got close, Caroline was surprised at how the buildings looked less like houses, and more like wooden huts. She realized that this was just a tiny village in the middle of the jungle. As she was marveling over this, she saw a man in the middle of the village waving his arms, jumping up and down, and screaming.

Getting closer and closer, Caroline saw that this man wasn't wearing a shirt, or shoes - in fact all he wore was a yellow grass skirt around his waist. And before she and Euni landed, dozens of other similarly dressed people began running toward the man, most of them pointing at Caroline and Euni while screaming frantically.

It was only then that Caroline realized what a sight she and Euni must be: a flying unicorn with a girl on its back coming out of the sky toward their remote jungle village.

"Let's be quick," Caroline nervously said to Euni.

"Eeee…"

When Caroline and Euni finally landed in the small village, the villagers circled around them, marveling at the spectacle. They chattered with one another in what sounded like a mixture of fear and awe, though Caroline couldn't understand a word they said. The women held tight to their children, most of whom hid, themselves terrified, behind the legs of the adults.

"Does anyone know which way to California?" Caroline asked tentatively, staying perched on top of Euni. She wiped beads of sweat from her forehead, surprised that it could be so hot in the middle of winter.

A man, naked except for his grass skirt, stepped forward. "Eres un dios o un demonio?" he called, loud enough so everyone around could hear.

"Uh oh," Caroline whispered. "We're nowhere near home."

"Qué clase de monstruo es este?" the same man yelled at Caroline, more aggressively, while pointing at Euni. The silence of all the other villagers told Caroline that this man was in charge.

"I… I don't understand," Caroline replied, getting nervous at the tone of the man's voice. "Do you… happen to speak… English?" She wiped her forehead again, amazed at the heat. She realized that they must be in the southern hemisphere, where the seasons were the opposite.

"*Euni Ama Ghee,*" Euni brayed softly. Caroline knew that Euni was saying she wanted to go.

The crowd around gasped at Euni's speech. Many of them took some fearful steps backward.

"Ay!" the man calling to Caroline yelped. Then he bellowed, "Dios o demonio!"

Caroline shook her head silently.

"Qué estás haciendo aquí?" the man yelled at Caroline.

"California?" Caroline asked anxiously, not knowing what else to say or do, and also suddenly wanting to leave. "United States?"

"Por qué estás aquí?" the man screamed, visibly angry now. He took a step toward Caroline and Euni.

Caroline looked down to Euni and reached her arms back over her broad white shoulders. "Okay time to go," she whispered to Euni.

"Bájate de esa bestia!" the man bellowed, and then reached toward Caroline's foot.

But one beat of Euni's giant wings knocked him back. The crowd gasped again and covered their faces. With a second beat of her wings Euni and Caroline were back in the air, and a few moments later the wind was firm in

Caroline's face as Euni sped through the sky away from the village.

Caroline looked to the morning sun and figured out which way was north. She knew that north was the direction they needed to go to get back to winter, and therefore, to get back home.

"Go that way," she yelled to Euni, pointing. Seeing how high the sun was getting in the sky, she added, "And fast!"

Chapter 28

Based on her sense of how much time had passed since their early morning escape from Misha, combined with the position of the sun in the sky, Caroline was growing more and more nervous about whether she would get home in time for her birthday party. She wasn't bothered by the possibility of missing her own birthday party, but she knew that if she wasn't home in time her father would be very worried or very angry - and probably both.

Caroline and Euni flew through the sky at an incredible speed. But as fast as Euni could fly, the problem really was whether they would be able to find their way home. Now feeling more or less confident that they were going in the right direction, away from the summer of the southern hemisphere toward the winter of their own northern hemisphere, Caroline was on the lookout for land.

"Let's turn a little to the right," Caroline told Euni as she put her jacket back on. "Let's at least find the coastline."

Feeling the chill in the air, Caroline was relieved that they were at least on the right side of the planet again. But Caroline still had no idea how fast they were flying. Based on how far they had traveled on the first flight, Euni was going far faster than an airplane - but how much faster?

Before they saw the coastline, they saw an enormous tornado-shaped cloud in the distance, like an upside-down triangle pointing to something on the ground below. The cloud was dark grey, the color of charcoal or ash, and as

Caroline and Euni flew closer they saw strikes of lightning inside and around it.

"I've never seen a storm like that," Caroline said. She felt a combination of curiosity and fear, and wondered whether Euni would avoid the storm or keep heading toward it - and her own curiosity stopped Caroline from telling Euni to change direction. She was especially curious about what was at the bottom of the storm, what could possibly be on the ground at the base of the huge grey funnel in the sky. And maybe Euni was curious too, for she kept flying directly toward the giant cloud.

But as they got closer rain began to fall, a bitter cold rain, and the booming of thunder began to fill their ears. "I think we shouldn't go any closer," Caroline finally said to Euni, her fear building along with her physical discomfort.

Without replying, Euni gently arced away from the storm cloud, and as she did, Caroline noticed some buildings, a town, a short distance from the base of the storm.

"There!" she cried, pointing. "Let's go see if they know where home is!" Still deeply curious, Caroline also wanted to ask the people in the town about the giant storm cloud. She just hoped they spoke English.

Caroline was also aware (this time!) that swooping down from the sky on the back of a flying unicorn wasn't the best way to make an introduction. So she told Euni to fly as low as she could, and to land in the trees on the outskirts of the town. From there, Caroline would walk into town on foot while Euni stayed behind, well hidden.

Flying lower, Caroline got a much better look at the area where the giant storm met the ground. At the bottom of the huge grey funnel cloud Caroline saw the base of a castle, a large stone castle with a moat, a drawbridge, and some cylindrical towers. It reminded her of the castles in the stories of King Arthur, the castles that held knights and queens and wizards inside. But the top of the castle, where she imagined there would be a tall tower, was completely hidden by the thick grey storm cloud. It gave Caroline the chills.

Soon Euni landed in a thicket of trees. It was still raining, but lighter here, away from the storm, and the castle. The air was also now bitter cold, a far cry from their last stop, so Caroline pulled her jacket tight around her body as she started the short walk toward the town.

Chapter 29

"She better be home soon," Caroline and Cora's father said to Cora from on top of a step stool.

Cora looked at the ground, bit her lip, and crossed her legs like she always did when very nervous.

"Party starts in an hour," he said, glancing at the clock.

"I think she'll be home by then," Cora said, still looking at the ground. She wondered if it was a lie to say that, because she wasn't sure she really believed it. "I mean, I hope so," she corrected herself. "And I also hope she's back with Euni, too." Cora looked up at her father and forced a small, hopeful smile.

"Tape please," her father said to Cora, who tore a piece of tape off a roll and handed it to him. He reached up and, able to touch the ceiling while standing on the step stool, used the tape to hang a dangling sparkly garland. "Euni or no, if Caroline isn't back soon… well, first, I'm not going to know what to say to all the guests coming." He looked down at Cora. "And second, most importantly, I'm going to start getting really worried."

Cora handed him another piece of tape, which he used to finish suspending the garland from the ceiling. "What will you say to the guests?" she asked.

Her father stepped down from the step stool and admired the decorations. The room was very festive, between the sparkly garlands, the paper rainbows and unicorns, and the huge Happy Birthday banner.

"I'm not sure yet," he said, walking back to the big cardboard box labeled *Birthday Decorations.* He pulled a colorful bag out of the box. "Let's blow up some balloons and then we can be done for now."

"Maybe that she's running late?" Cora said, shrugging.

The two of them sat on the couch and inflated balloons. Cora's were small, and she needed help tying them, while the ones her father inflated were huge. Cora cringed every time he filled a balloon, nervous that they were going to pop in his face (and a couple times they did!).

"I think I need to trust her," he said after they finished, now surrounded by a small sea of red, yellow, pink, and blue balloons. "She's a responsible girl. She said she'd be home. She goes into the forest all the time. And I'm just going to trust, for now, that she'll be home in time."

Even if he didn't say so to Cora, her father did think to himself, "What if," and felt a wave of anxiety. But he reminded himself that even before the arrival of Euni, Caroline would spend hours exploring the forest by herself. That was, after all, how she found Euni, or the rainbow frog. And in all those times, Caroline had never been late coming home.

"Why don't you go play for a while, Cora," her father said, "while I finish getting ready."

Cora stomped her foot. "But… but I want to help. And, Carolyn…"

"Okay, okay. How about, you go see if you can find Caroline in the forest. Don't go farther than the creek of course, but that's how you can help. Help me make sure she's back in time for her party."

Chapter 30

Caroline wished she was wearing a watch. "I don't know what time it is," she whispered to herself as she walked out of the woods and into the small town. "But I guess it doesn't matter. I just need to hurry."

The town was a scattered collection of wood homes, all looking more or less the same, with the exception of the large building in the center of town. That building was much taller than the rest, and much darker. The top of it looked like a clocktower or the spire of a church, and if not for the ugly charcoal color Caroline would have assumed it was a church.

As she walked toward the large building, Caroline realized that it wasn't just a different color than the other buildings - it was burned. The whole building was charred, and the dark tower seemed to barely stay standing, while much of the large roof that extended from the tower over the building was caved in.

Caroline frowned, and recognized the smell of burned wood in the air. It reminded her of campfires, and the smell they left on her clothes. That in turn reminded her of her father, and the campfires he made, and of roasting marshmallows with him - and her frown deepened.

Then Caroline realized, suddenly, how eerily quiet the town was. "Where is everyone?" she thought to herself. The houses weren't burned down. They looked fine, somehow totally untouched by the fire.

"Hello!" Caroline yelled, and then listened to the echo of her voice. Where were the birds? Or other animals? "Hello?"

She eventually heard a rustling noise in one of the nearby homes. "Hello?" she said again toward the home, though not as loud this time, and more a question. She walked toward the home. "Anybody there?"

"Whaddya want?" a gruff voice said.

Caroline couldn't see where it came from, and the angry tone of the voice scared her. "But at least I understand what it said," she thought.

"I… I'm lost," Caroline called out. No one answered. "I just need help… finding my way home."

There was a murmur of multiple voices from the direction of the first one. "An argument," Caroline thought, "between the gruff voice and the voice of a woman."

Then she heard the woman's voice say, "She's just a small girl!" And then the woman, a plump blonde woman in a faded flower dress, stepped out from the house.

"Hullo dearie," the woman said, in a funny but friendly accent. "Perhaps I can be of hulp. Where is your hoom? Because you don't sound like you're from around here."

"Um… California?" Caroline said tentatively.

The woman's eyes widened. "Califoornia?" she said, amazed.

"Do you know where that is?" Caroline asked, feeling hopeful.

"Sure I know where 'tis, but, but how did you get here?"

A stocky man with a very large beard hanging down in front of a very large belly came out of the same home, and was followed by three kids who stared fearfully at Caroline. "I told you!" he said to the woman in his gruff voice. He was clearly the man who first yelled to Caroline. "I told you, she's with the witch! It's either magic, or a trick! Maybe she is the witch! And now, now what do you suppose we do, eh?"

"A witch?" Caroline gasped. "No! I'm no witch! And I don't know any magic." Caroline wondered to herself whether flying unicorns counted as magic.

"Then what might you be doing here?" the man screamed at Caroline. "A bit far from hoom, ain't ya?"

"I...I..." Caroline hated to be yelled at, had been yelled at far too much that day, and really all she wanted to do was get home. She started crying, overwhelmed and saddened. "I just want to go home," she sniveled.

"What's your name, dearie?" the woman asked gently.

"Caroline." Tears flowed down her cheeks.

"Wull my name is Roberta, and this here is Robert," the woman said. "Nice to meet you Caroline. Now, I can tell you, Caroline, that California is that way." The woman pointed. "Directly south," she said.

"It is?" Caroline said, eyes wide, and nearly jumping in excitement and relief.

"But," the woman continued, "it's a thousand miles, that way."

"And how, exactly, will you get there?" the gruff man, Robert, said. "Magic, I imagine?"

Caroline didn't know what to say, or what not to say, to avoid more trouble for herself. But now that she knew the direction of home, she considered whether she could just run from the town, back into the woods, and fly away with Euni like they had on their last stop, and the one before.

So Caroline, ready to start running, turned around back toward the forest where Euni was hiding. Only then did she realize that dozens of other townspeople had come out of their homes to see Caroline and to listen to the conversation. And these townspeople formed a wall, of sorts, that blocked Caroline's path back to Euni.

Caroline started crying again, just as hard as prior to her brief moments of hope.

Chapter 31

"I don't know any witch," Caroline said with a sniffle, turning back toward Robert and Roberta but looking at the ground.

"What else would a witch say?" Robert grumbled.

Then, amidst her tears, and her exhausted fear - amidst her feeling all the pressures from the day, along with her lack of sleep, and utter hopelessness - Caroline had an idea.

She looked up at Robert, straight into his eyes, and asked, "Is it the witch that burned down your church?"

Townspeople murmured behind her. Robert and Roberta looked toward their charred church, and frowned.

"Aye," Robert said softly.

"That's terrible," Caroline said. "Was anyone hurt?"

"She's an evil witch!" Robert yelled. "Er, you're an evil witch!" He was upset but had grown slightly confused.

"Now you can see, dearie" Roberta said to Caroline, "why we're so worried. Fortunately, no, no one was hurt. But the witch is why we hide. And don't trust."

"Why did she do it?" Caroline asked.

"Why!" Robert yelled, suddenly quite angry again. "What kind of question it that? Because she's evil! Don't you listen, little girl?"

Caroline was actually wondering why the witch burned only the one building down, and not the whole town. And why she burned down the church, while not hurting anyone.

And why it happened when it did, since, assuming she lived in the nearby castle, the witch had been living near the town for quite a while, probably from the time the town was first built.

But Caroline didn't ask any of these more specific questions, because Robert was still yelling at her. "She's a witch! With magic and storms! Lightning, and unicorns! Only a mutter of time before she returns to finish the job!"

Caroline startled at his mention of unicorns. "There were other unicorns?" she thought to herself. "With an evil witch?" But instead of asking any more questions, feeling like time was running out, and seeing an opportunity in Robert not referring to her as the witch anymore, Caroline said: "Maybe I can help."

"Hulp?" Robert scoffed. "You? A little girl, hulp us?" He stood up strong and straight.

Roberta elbowed him in the stomach. "Hear her out," she told Robert. "What's the harm now?"

"Let me go back into the forest from where I came from," Caroline said, "and I'll come up with a plan to help you. A plan to save you from the witch." She had no idea what her plan could be, but she also found herself wondering if the witch, a witch with unicorns, could really be as bad as they said. Caroline also assumed, hopefully, that her father would have some ideas.

Townspeople all around began whispering to one another. "Could she really?" Caroline heard some say amid the murmuring. Robert glared at Caroline, his anger now visibly mixed with doubt.

"Wull," Roberta said with a smile. "No harm letting her go, Robert. Magic or no."

Robert grunted, and kept his eyes on Caroline.

"Think about it, Robert," Roberta said. "If the girl was going to hurt us, she'd have already tried. I mean, why not? And if she was with the witch, or is the witch, why the pretending? What did she accomplish? Nuthin. But maybe, Robert, maybe she could hulp, no? Maybe, especially if she does have magic? So, best to only show our good sides, eh, Robert? Show her how kind, and how peace loving, we are?"

Robert grumbled loudly before walking back into his house, his three children following him closely.

"We're going to take your word, dearie," Roberta said to Caroline, smiling kindly. "Aye, do we need hulp. And maybe your magic shall hulp us. We're friendly people, y'see. All of us, gentle and loving people. Peaceful people who'll be awaiting your return, dearie."

As the townspeople slowly began to scatter, Caroline ran back into the forest and found Euni lying right where she left her. *"Carolynnn!"* Euni brayed. *"Ghee Hitimi?"*

Caroline smiled widely as she climbed onto Euni's back. "Yes, Euni, let's go home. That way," she said, pointing. "And while we're flying, I have quite the story to tell you!"

Chapter 32

"Where's Caroline and Cora?" Caroline's friend and classmate, Todd, asked their father. "I haven't even seen the birthday girl yet!"

"They'll be here soon," Caroline and Cora's father said with a forced smile. "Now go keep playing with the other kids. We have lots of games and snacks, so go have fun!"

Todd ran off, back to the area of the backyard full of arts and crafts.

"At least, they better be here soon," their father grumbled to himself, checking his watch. "Gerald's gonna be here with the cake any minute…"

"Hey there buddy!" One of the adults, a father of another friend of Caroline's, came and shook Caroline and Cora's father's hand while slapping him on the back. "Quite a party, nice work man."

"Thank you."

"I gotta ask though, what's this big animal pen here? Looks like quite the project."

"Yeah, it was. Caroline wanted a unicorn house, and I thought it would be a fun way to teach her how things are built."

The man laughed. "A unicorn house! Awesome. With a bed and all! Incredible. Quite an imagination on that girl. Speaking of which, where is the birthday girl?"

"She's coming," her father said. "She's coming."

And, indeed, Caroline was coming. Soaring through the air on Euni's back, in the direction Roberta had shown her,

Caroline soon recognized the landscape of northern California. Between her airplane trips and her love of maps and geography, Caroline was able to figure out where they were, and then exactly where they needed to go to get home.

As they flew, Caroline anxiously hoped that she was back in time for her party. If she missed her party it was going to be a disaster, for several reasons - reasons that Caroline, after how her birthday had gone so far, didn't want to think about.

Meanwhile, after hearing of Caroline's encounter with the townspeople, and about the burned down church and the evil witch and the witch's unicorns, Euni was busy thinking about these other unicorns. She wondered who they were, if they looked like her, and if they were related to her. She also wondered why in the world they would be with an evil witch.

While Caroline and Euni were flying, Cora was standing alone by the creek, throwing rocks, waiting hopefully for her sister's return. Every now and then she'd call out, "Carolyn!!!" but there was never any answer. She grew more and more worried, both about Caroline and about what was happening back at the birthday party - the party for the girl who wasn't there.

"Let's land there!" Caroline said, spotting the creek. "And let's make sure no one sees us, same as before."

Euni slowed down, gently swooping toward the familiar trees in the familiar forest behind Caroline and Cora's house.

As they approached, Caroline saw Cora moping near the creek. "Cora!!" Caroline hollered from just above the trees. She was overwhelmed with excitement and relief to see her little sister.

Cora began jumping up and down. "Carolyn!!! Yay, Carolyn!"

Right when Euni landed Caroline jumped off, and the two sisters ran to one another and gave each other an enormous, warm embrace. "I'm so happy to see you," they each said at the same time, followed by a sisterly giggle.

After the long hug, Cora looked back at Euni. "Carolyn," she said, confused. "How did Euni... those wings... where..."

"I'll explain later, Cora. I promise," Caroline said. "But tell me, is the party over? Please, please tell me it isn't."

"I hope not!" Cora said, smiling. Then she grabbed Caroline by the hand and yelled, "Let's go!"

Back at Caroline's birthday party, a large man in a white chef's outfit came out of the house, into the backyard, carrying an enormous white cake. The cake was three tiers tall, with rainbows decorating the edges, and ten candles flickering on the top next to some small figurines.

"Oh no," Caroline and Cora's father said, seeing what was happening. The man carrying the cake was Gerald, Caroline and Cora's father's friend who was a baker, and always insisted on baking a cake for the girls' birthdays - which the girls learned to insist on, as well.

In a deep, booming voice, Gerald began singing: "Haaaaaappy biiiirthday to yooooou!"

Everyone at the party joined in, even while many of them began looking around for the person they were singing to.

"Haaaaappy birthday toooo yooooooooou!"

Caroline and Cora's father panicked, wanting to stop the singing and the cake. But he saw that he was too late, the song half done, the cake almost to the special table - the special table with an empty chair in front of it, the chair where Caroline was supposed to be sitting.

"Haaappy birthday deeeeear Caroliiiiine!"

"Oh no oh on oh no," their father mumbled, shaking his head, not knowing what to do. He placed his hand on his forehead, partially covering his eyes.

"Haaaappy biiiiiirthdayyyy…" Gerald placed the enormous cake down on the table. On the top of the cake was a candy unicorn next to a candy girl in a pink heart dress who looked just like Caroline.

"Toooooo…" seeing the empty chair at the table, Gerald joined the rest of the guests in looking around, confused, in search of the birthday girl.

They finished the song anyway. "Yoooooooooooou!!!"

"Yay!" a cheer came from the edge of the forest - the cheer of two joyous sisters.

All the guests, along with Caroline and Cora's father, looked over and saw the two girls skipping happily, hand-in-hand, toward the cake.

Without missing a beat, Caroline skipped to the edge of the cake, closed her eyes as she made a wish, and then blew out each and every one of the candles.

Gasps of "wow," "whoa," "oooh," and "awesome," erupted from the group of kids crowded around.

"What an entrance!" one of the adults shouted.

"On my birthday can I do it like that too?" one girl asked her parents.

"Amazing," exclaimed another adult.

Caroline and Cora's father drew in a deep breath, and then sighed heavily. "Yeah," he said to himself. "Amazing."

He shook his head, but couldn't help smiling.

THE END

"Let's go see about that witch!"

Thank you for reading!

Like the book?
Don't forget to leave a review on Amazon
to let others know, and share the word!

Stay tuned for more books in the Caroline and Euni Series.

Visit JSJoseph.com to:
learn about how this book (and the next 140
chapters, and counting!) came about;
to see all the illustrations in color;
and to sign up to find out about future books!

Email Joshua with any questions, comments or
feedback:
Joshua@JSJoseph.com
Instagram: @ThisIsJoshuaJ

And Email Chia with any feedback on his
illustrations or inquiries for further work:
chiaamerico@gmail.com
Instagram: @chia_americo

Made in the USA
Las Vegas, NV
13 November 2020